CHARMED BY HIS LORDSHIP

JEN GEIGLE JOHNSON

ALL OF REGENCY HOUSE PARTY
HAVENCREST

Miss Marleigh's Pirate
The Vexatious Widow
Charmed by His Lordship
The Captain's Lady
The Marriage Bargain

FOLLOW JEN

.

Jen has five other published books

The Nobleman's Daughter
Two lovers in disguise

Scarlet
The Pimpernel retold

Spun of Gold
Rumplestilskin Retold

Dating the Duke
Time Travel: Regency man in NYC

Tabitha's Folly
Four over protective Brothers

To read Damen's Secret
The Villain's Romance

Follow her Newsletter

CHAPTER 1

A family could only afford one do-nothing wastrel, and Lord Abraham Bolton's brother had secured that role long ago. A certain feeling of doom settled across Abraham's shoulders as he stared out across the ocean, the white cliffs towering above him in ominous observance of his task: to woo and marry a woman of substantial dowry. The wind on the Brighton beach whipped through his hair, but he gave it no mind. His valet would have him presented to perfection when he returned to his room. He let out the tension in his chest through one large breath after another. So much of his future success rode on this one house party.

Loud giggling carried over to him on the wind, and he was reminded of a persistent woman he'd met in London one month past. Another burst of laughter and a feminine exclamation, and he felt sure of its owner. Out of the corner of his eye, her figure came into view, and he groaned. Miss Margaret Tittering. And her intrusive guardian, Mrs. Harrow. Praise be, her guardian was at least present. Miss Tittering had spent the whole of one London ball trying to sequester him in a corner. A forced tie to her would not be endurable, dowry or no.

Her excited chatter grew nearer.

He froze. If he ran, she'd surely see him. Carefully positioning himself so that he faced completely away from the pair of them, he held his breath.

"Lord Bolton!" Her shout sounded small, wispy enough he could ignore it. Desperately he searched the beach for a diversion, something, anything; for he knew she would call his name again, and then he'd be relied upon to acknowledge her and escort them.

A lone figure, a woman in a white dress, with a full bonnet covering any view of her face, walked along the water's edge. Perfect. He moved in her direction, picking up his pace when he heard another call of his name.

At last arriving at her side, he bowed to speak to the side of her head in urgent undertones. "Please, miss, this will seem so untoward, but I am in need of your assistance."

Her head swung in his direction so fast she nipped his eye with the rim of her bonnet.

"Ah. Oh, ow, woman, you've sliced me in the eye." Tears poured from his eye and it stung, a desperate need to blink plaguing him.

She sniffed and turned away. "Well, if you hadn't come upon me in such a brash manner, and we not even introduced, I imagine your eye would have been spared."

Miss Tittering moved closer. He could hear her and almost smell her intense scent of rose, always too much rose. With one hand over his still suffering eye, he began again. "I know we don't know one another, but I am in need of some assistance. If you wouldn't mind pretending as if we were acquainted?"

Her eyes lifted to his, and he was struck by the brightness of the blue staring back at him. Her pert nose wrinkled; her lips thinned. She looked as though she would turn away again, but he held out his arm. "Please. Might we suppose we are dear friends, and I have agreed to escort you and catch up on our mothers." She eyed him with disdain, but a tiny flicker of adventure danced across her expression, and he knew he had a chance. "Please, take my arm? Perhaps you are in need of your chaperone? We can go to her forthwith."

"I don't know what to say. It's all highly improper, and my chaper-one, you are most correct I have one—Mrs. Dotting is her name—is not even here to advise me." She eyed him with no small amount of suspicion.

He gave her his most charming smile and waited. "I am in the most desperate need."

Her mouth twitched, and she placed a gloved hand over her lips to hide what he hoped was a smile. "Oh, I suppose there is no harm in it." She placed a hand on his arm. "There. Now will you tell me what this is all about? I've never met the likes of you." Her fingers trembled on his arm. How young a creature had he imposed himself upon? Tendrils of guilt disturbed his peace, but before addressing any wrong to his new accomplice, he must rid himself of other annoyances.

Miss Tittering approached with her companion not far behind, her face red from the exertion of walking across the tiny rocks that made up the beaches in Brighton. "Lord Bolton! I knew it was you. What a delight, what pure enjoyment will be ours. Imagine both of us here in Brighton at the same time."

Before she could make a move to attach herself to his other arm, he bowed, "Miss Tittering. Mrs. Harrow." He dipped his head to them both. "I too am surprised at our being here the same week. Imagine. Standing on the same rocks." He turned to his companion, the side of her bonnet all he could make out as far as her expression. "I would like to introduce a Miss, eh . . . Bumbly."

She gasped and turned to him, her mouth wide. He searched her youthful expression. He'd wager she was just out of the school room if out in society at all. But what seemed like a stubborn streak to her personality told him she might not let youth or innocence deter a setting down in response to his personal affront to her name and privacy.

He winked. "And Miss Bumbly, this is Miss Tittering and Mrs. Harrow."

The three ladies curtseyed, and he bowed. "Lovely day to take a stroll, but Miss Tittering, Mrs. Harrow, I do feel that apologies are in order, for I've just been given the task of accompanying this young lady, the ward of a friend . . ."

Her fingers tightened on his arm.

"To her chaperone. You've happened upon us quite at the moment of our departure. I'm sure you understand." His eye started to sting again, and he wiped at it.

Miss Tittering eyed him in suspicion. "Lord Bolton, are you ill?"

"He is abominably ill-used." The surprisingly wicked raise of Miss Bumbly's eyebrow held Lord Bolton's attention.

Then he coughed. "Pardon?"

"Yes, attacked." She nodded to the others, the decisive rise of her chin, at once powerful and charming.

He forced a straight face. "Attacked . . ."

"By a seagull."

The ladies gasped and searched the air in alarm.

"The evil bird came at him while he was searching the sky for . . . um, rain." She looked away, her mouth twitching furiously.

All Abraham could do was stare in amazement.

"Until it dropped a bit of something right inside."

The ladies stepped back with expressions of disgust.

Aghast at the thought, he shook his head. "That did not . . ."

She lifted her hand and tilted her head in warning.

He coughed. "Did not surprise me in the least, for this beach has the most vicious and intrusive birds." He searched the empty sky again for one. "And now, if you'll excuse us? I must get this young lady back to those who care for her." He dipped his head and led the lady away toward the house. He would thank the seas she came with him, her tiny hand still gracing his arm and her small frame in step beside him.

When they were sure to be alone, she sniffed. "Do you find your-self in this situation often? In need of subterfuge to rid yourself of unwanted women?" Her face was completely blank, and he couldn't tell if she disapproved. Though he suspected her opinion of him not too high.

"A seagull? Leaving dropping in my eye? Come now."

"I felt it fitting."

"I do thank you for your timely assistance. How pleasurable for me to discover someone as lovely as you to hide me." He grinned, hoping she would turn her head again so that he might look into her face, but he kept his distance, already the victim of her bonnet rim.

Thinking of it caused his eyes to water once again.

"Do take this if you must wipe at your eye incessantly." She handed him a lace handkerchief.

He dipped his head. "I thank you. It does sting a bit." The gift smelled of a lovely mix of oranges and lemons. "Much better. And now I'm in your debt twofold."

"I admit I assumed your need truly dire, as you communicated." She sniffed. "Though I'm unconvinced it is precisely as you say."

"My situation is dire indeed. Has she gone?"

The woman glanced up the beach. "No." Then she turned from him and huffed. "Miss Bumbly? I cannot even remember how to say it correctly. Is Bumbly to be my new name? Someone's ward?"

He did not blame her for her disapproval. But he must continue to beg her good will. "I didn't know what to do. What recourses were left to me, we not yet introduced?"

Her chin rose higher and her eyes flashed. "I refuse to allow you to be the victim. You have come upon me, begged my help, changed my identity and reduced me to the status of someone's ward."

"I shall make amends, I promise, but first, I believe we must carry on a little longer? Has she gone?"

"Still no."

"Then I'm afraid I must beg to trespass more upon your kindness. For we must continue to seem as though we are quite fond of one another." He turned to face her, stepping as close as he dared to the skittish miss. "Like so. Now, if you would, look up into my face as though I'm important to you."

She brushed a hair from her face and then fisted her hand. He was impressed with her fire. But as she tipped up her bonnet, her eyes wide, he nearly stepped back at the innocence that stared back. She eyed him for a moment and then asked, "Like this?"

Enchanting, with the full force of her face looking up into his. He'd rarely met such a beauty. Who was this woman? She was youthful, yes, but as he studied the curve of her beautiful neckline, the softness of her skin, the curve of her lips, he saw nothing of the child. He breathed. "Excellent. Just so. And now I will move my hand to adjust this one curl, here." He waited for her to nod her acceptance, and then he moved it out of her face, enjoying the soft feel of her skin just skimming against his fingers. The errant curl held its perfectly coiled shape.

"Oh." Her face flushed.

"Have you had a season?"

She nodded. "Just one, but it was cut short, you see, else I'd be married now, surely. That's the way it is done, is it not?" She seemed flustered.

He stepped back. "I don't hear her any longer. Would you mind causally gazing about the beach and tell me if they are close?"

She blinked and turned her head. He held back a laugh at her overly large attempt to appear indifferent. Then she nodded. "They are still here." She straightened. "I feel I have spent enough time with you alone on this beach. Mrs. Dotting should have been here by now. She is my chaperone, if you remember."

He held out his arm. "I am greatly in your debt. I thank you for your kindness, for you have saved me from a lengthy and uncomfortable encounter. I'd be happy to continue in my escort to find her?"

She raised her eyebrows. "Your uncomfortable encounter has been avoided, yet you have gifted me my own. It is all so very untoward. I don't quite know what to do. Nothing in the books, not even my governess has prepared me for the likes of you." Her cheeks colored again, and he was charmed.

"The likes of me? And how exactly would you describe the likes of me?" He had immediately found a most diverting activity in unsettling his beautiful new companion.

"Oh, you are too much. Which is precisely your measure. Too much. Too improper, too reckless. Untoward." She gasped. "They warned me against men such as you."

He laughed again, completely fascinated by her. "I imagine they did." Then a worry crept in. She'd been warned against men such as his brother, but he, Abraham, was a harmless flirt, not a do-nothing, gambling waste of a human. He'd heard himself described as a jovial nature, a fun associate, a flirt, for years. He was, wasn't he? He paused to consider his actions. Perhaps not to this woman, in this instance. Perhaps he would need to amend her opinion of him. As soon as he avoided Miss Tittering completely.

They walked a minute more, Abraham wishing they could linger, but her steps were hurried. "Let me ask you this. Was our encounter enjoyable?"

She started to nod and then stiffened. "That hardly signifies, as I doubt very much it was proper."

"Oh, but it wasn't *im*proper. There are so many delightful activities that fall right in that area of not proper but not terribly improper either." He stood taller. "Because I *am* of the proper sort. Though at times my activities might diverge into the questionable but not improper."

She sniffed. "I think I shall manage my actions so as to stay well within those defined as decidedly proper."

He laughed and steadied her as they made their way. "Then you might miss the magic. And we can't have that. Take this morning, for example . . ."

A matronly looking woman, red in the face, hurried towards them, her hands in a flurry, her bonnet attempting to fly away in the wind, tendrils of her hair blowing out about her face.

"That is Mrs. Dotting."

"Your chaperone?"

"Yes, and she doesn't look pleased."

"Before she arrives and unsettles things, consider carefully. If we kept ourselves so decidedly within staid lines of your chaperone's creation, I would have missed spending time with you." He dipped his head so as to be within sight from within the walls of her rather large and dangerous bonnet. "I've been enchanted. I shall never accept time with such an exquisite creature to be a crime."

Her mouth opened, her eyes wide. She said nothing, but he saw a hint of the daring, a hint that told him she would be an engaging conquest, a truly diverting flirtation.

Mrs. Dotting approached. "Oh, my lady, my dear. I apologize for my delay." She bustled her way in between the two of them and eyed him with the greatest suspicion.

She was titled? Again he cursed his brother's reckless behavior that such a thing should matter in the search for a wife. He bowed his most gallant effort. "I thank you for your time this fine morning. Perhaps we shall some day truly meet?"

Mrs. Dotting gasped. "You've not been introduced. Oh my dear." She eyed Abraham and her charge.

Highly amused, Abraham watched the guilt take over his accomplice's face, but as her eyes flitted to his, that same adventurous glint dared him to pursue the diversions they could have together. Alas, he could not. So he nodded. "Thank you. I've had an enlightening morning."

She bustled away, chattering with Mrs. Dotting toward the very stairs he would ascend. Could it be? Were they to attend the same house party? He watched them unabashedly until they were almost out of sight and was rewarded with a glance over her shoulder in his direction.

Triumphantly, he raised his arm in response. She whipped her head back to the front so quickly, he had to laugh. She was diverting. And certainly completely unavailable to him.

CHAPTER 2

elicity Honora Honeyfield had never felt so discomfited in her life. The wind blew her hair, but it stayed nicely secured beneath her bonnet. The rocks were uneven and shifted beneath her feet, but she walked with steady ease toward the path leading up to the Garveys' house party. Her gloves remained glaringly white. Her skirts fell precisely to the tops of her slippers. Everything appeared to be under control. But she could do nothing about her heart's rebellious, erratic beat. She could do nothing for the strange upheaval she'd never experienced before. The man's shocking behavior should have horrified her. And yet.

Mrs. Dotting's constant looks in her direction were not helping. They hurried together up the beach toward the path to the house. Felicity resisted looking in any other direction and resisted wondering what more had happened to a certain man who she hoped not to notice ever again. Did he watch their progress across the beach?

She clasped her hands to her front, steadying her steps as she walked. "We must greet our hostess; I believe it is high time." When their carriage had arrived, she had wanted a brief respite with the ocean air all about her after so many hours of travel. She expected the walk to restore her constitution, but instead she was . . . unsettled was the best way to describe her current state . . . and unsure. Her stomach clenched in an upheaval not altogether unpleasant, but not at all calm.

She shook off the tingling sensation on the back of her hand where he'd pressed his lips and marched with purpose across the rest of the steep incline to do her duty to Mrs. Garvey, the hostess. Did he watch her? Every part of her awoke in awareness of movement, conscious of the rise of her shoulders, of the fall of her feet. If he watched, what did he see? She resisted turning her head, though her body burned with the sensation of being watched, the pleasant awareness of alluring eyes, friendly curiosity, interest. She and Mrs. Dotting stepped on the first of the stone stairs, leading back up to the house. Five more steps to a turn in the stairwell, and Felicity would turn out of sight of the beach. What if she never saw him again? Did he watch her still? She risked a glance over her shoulder, and when his hand raised in farewell, she gasped, and then a sudden giggle shocked her in its escape from her own lips. Mrs. Dotting eyed her in alarm.

"I'm sure you think the worst of me, Mrs. Dotting, accompanied by a man, alone, but I assure you, I was a complete victim to the outlandish behavior of that man. We were on our way, directly to find you."

Her chaperone fanned her face. "It was I who am at fault. If only I'd gathered my wits sooner to attend you."

"I believe we are well, reputations still intact, and perfectly suited to begin our efforts with Lord Ridgecrest. You do remember the purpose of this visit?" She asked to reassure herself as much as her chaperone. Something about the outlandish man on the beach had her quivering in a manner she had not experienced. A good reminder of who the perfect man in her life was meant to be, namely Lord Ridgecrest, would aid in dousing any girlish fancies about men with completely uncouth ideas and fascinating eyes. Fordyce's sermons had warned her of just such a thing.

"Of course, my lady." Her chaperone hurried beside her, breath coming faster. The woman's roundness was quite charming, but it made traversing a rocky path at a faster pace challenging. She breathed out. "Will we be meeting the Garveys?"

"Yes, straight away. My stomach is settled. The good sea air has helped considerably." Though in actuality she felt far from settled. She wasn't sure what to do about the lingering upheaval and flutterings traversing her whole frame, but she hoped she would never see the likes of that man again.

They approached the house. It was a lovely estate. She was looking forward to the tour and had heard it acclaimed far and wide. Though she'd heard mixed reactions of the host and hostess. To some they were the most magnanimous, and to others miserable misers.

"Lord Ridgecrest. He will arrive at the party shortly. We must keep our eye fixated on our purpose here, Mrs. Dotting. We must position ourselves, give him every opportunity to express an interest."

"Yes, my lady. I can imagine he would be amenable to an alliance. Especially when he remembers your father, his familial connections to your mother." She sniffed. "Besides the obvious, that you're perfectly lovely and have a respectable dowry."

"Perhaps best not to mention my mother at first." A twinge of shame made her swallow twice over the lump that rose in her throat.

"Your mother was the best of women."

"I know, and you know. But not everyone knows, do they?" She hoped that the Ridgecrests were those who did appreciate her mother. Lord Ridgecrest should, at any rate, if only for gratitude's sake.

The approach to the home was fine, lovely, and well cared for, reminding Felicity of her own questionable lineage by comparison. "I am a lady," she murmured.

"What was that?" Mrs. Dotting eyed her again with rising concern.

"It is nothing. Just reminding myself I belong here as much as anyone."

"That you do." Mrs. Dotting's kind hand on her arm comforted as much as it annoyed. She didn't need the sympathy of others. Or perhaps she did. What a mess her emotions were as they whipped around inside. They approached the front door, and the butler answered.

She lifted her chin. "Lady Felicity Honora Honeyfield and Mrs. Dotting."

He stepped back to allow entrance. "Welcome. I believe your carriage arrived earlier?"

"Yes, and I do thank you for helping our things get settled?"

"You will find everything in your room, which is down the first wing and to the right. Your servants have been directed to their accommodations as well."

She nodded. "And where might we find Mrs. Garvey?" She wished to do her duty to her hostess and become acquainted with such a talked-of individual. She heard such varying reports of the woman, she wondered what her own opinion would be. She and Mrs. Dotting were led to the front room. The footman announced, "Lady Felicity Honora Honeyfield. Mrs. Dotting. Of Haversham."

She curtseyed precisely, delicately, and kept her eyes down in her most demure expression. Everyone in the room stood. As she looked up from her own curtsey, she met the eyes of Lord Ridgecrest in the middle of his bow. *He is here.* His eyes raised in recognition, and he nodded.

"Did you see that?" Felicity hissed through her smiling teeth, her heart hammering. "He nodded at us."

"Good, he remembers the acquaintance. That will make introductions less awkward and hopefully unnecessary."

Her hands shook, not knowing how to function in a normal manner when one's happiness relied so much upon simple and fickle things like catching a gentleman's eye. He was already entertaining two women. Many women through the ton had their eye on him, she was sure. But not many had her connection to him. Perhaps he would notice the power of fate working its tendrils on their behalf. . .

But how to situate herself closer? Her gaze swept the room. She was almost too long in the entry. So often her governess had reprimanded, *If you must be the center of attention, do not linger.*

She smiled and rested a hand on Mrs. Dotting's arm. She murmured, "Stay close. Remember you are to watch for any hint of impropriety in me." So often, she wondered who was chaperoning who. She wanted someone to keep everything on the up and up.

And Mrs. Dotting was just such a person, though forgetful, unfortunately always needing to be reminded of her duties. Felicity would have never even had a run-in with that mysterious man at the beach at all if Mrs. Dotting had been present.

She and Mrs. Dotting were soon settled in a settee near enough to Lord Ridgecrest that she could overhear his conversations on one side and quite close enough for a conversation with a pair of ladies on her other side.

One, lovely, friendly looking woman of striking auburn hair greeted them immediately. "I'm so happy you've come to join us. We were just about out of interesting topics." She fanned herself. "And I for one dread boredom. Do tell me all about yourself, please."

Felicity was immediately taken aback. For one, she had never been introduced to this friendly person. Though they had announced Felicity and Mrs. Dotting to the room, she didn't feel that sufficient enough acquaintance to begin a conversation with her.

Lord Ridgecrest joined them, as if he sensed her trouble. "Allow me." He bowed to them both. "For I am so fortunate as to be acquainted with the both of you. And we would stave off boredom whenever we can." He winked. Felicity warmed in gratitude. He was already anticipating her needs. He held his hand out for the other woman to take. "Miss Melanie Tanning, I would like to introduce you to an old friend, Lady Felicity."

Felicity Honeyfield wished Lord Ridgecrest had taken *her* hand. Her gaze traveled between the two. Though Miss Tanning's face held a hint of a flush, that could just as easily have been from the over exuberance in which she'd greeted Felicity. "I am so pleased to make your acquaintance, Miss Tanning, and to see you again,

16

Lord Ridgecrest. It's been an age, and I am certain we have much to discuss to reacquaint one another."

He nodded. "I'm sure we do."

Another man approached. Felicity recognized again her great disadvantage at knowing so few people. He bowed. "If introductions are to be made to these charming women, I'd love to become acquainted as well." His eyes travelled over Felicity's face, and she warmed under his friendly perusal of her person. She smiled and gave him her hand.

"This is the lovely Lady Felicity and Miss Tanning. And this gentleman comes to us straight from London, a Mr. Cavanaugh at your service, I'm sure."

Did Felicity catch a hint of irony? But she could see nothing untoward in their expressions. She stood and curtseyed, pleased for this opportunity so soon to converse with Lord Ridgecrest up close. She cleared her throat, addressing Mr. Cavanaugh. "Has the weather been nice?"

"Oh, delightful. I've already taken a turn on the beach. We've visited the pier in Brighton and taken a turn on the Old Steine. The Royal Pavilion is looking more complete in its construction and it is a sight. It has been lovely and diverting." Mr. Cavanaugh held out his arm. "I'd be happy to return with you if you'd like. I'm sure our hosts will have a planned visit as well. Would you do me the honor now of a turn about the room? Perhaps more introductions are in order as well as an opportunity to hear how it is you might know our Lord Ridgecrest so well?"

Lord Ridgecrest cleared his throat, and she caught his subtle shake of the head. She nodded with a small smile. And already they shared a secret. "Oh, it is nothing so very interesting. We were childhood friends."

"Ah, so you might have information as to his childhood, which sticks were best for swordplay and the like?" Mr. Cavanaugh led her away.

"I'm afraid our connections were limited, but I will say he was a lovely companion at dropping sticks in the river."

Mr. Cavanaugh laughed overly loud, and Felicity at once questioned her association with him. A glance at Mrs. Dotting did nothing to help her. The woman was already deep in conversation with Miss Tanning's companion, who she'd not yet been introduced to either.

At about halfway round the room, the footman entered again and announced, "Lord Abraham Bolton of London."

She gasped, and Mr. Cavanaugh glanced at her curiously. When she arose from her curtsey, she tried desperately to keep her coloring normal.

"Do you know him?"

"I—well—no." She lifted her lashes to him. "I cannot explain my reaction."

He chuckled. "Well, unfortunately for the rest of us, Lord Bolton has that effect on most women. Come, I'll get you an introduction."

She wanted to dig her slippers into the floor. "No, it's quite all right . . ."

"Lord Bolton, someone desires your acquaintance."

Her man from the beach turned, an expectant and polite expression on his face until he saw Felicity, and then his face lit in delight. "Does she now?" The amusement in his eyes made Felicity want to turn from him, but she held her place, not daring to perform such an affront. Instead of speaking at all, she curtseyed while Mr. Cavanaugh said, "Lady Felicity, might I present Lord Abraham Bolton, an old friend from Oxford, and a decent chap besides."

Felicity held out her hand. "A pleasure."

"Oh, Lady Felicity. The pleasure is mine, naturally." He bowed over her hand, and the pressure of his lips once again on the same knuckle did strange things to her insides. He released her hand all too soon. "Perhaps we shall get to know one another during today's events?"

"I'm certain we shall."

He bowed. "As I see you are in the excellent hands of my friend Cavanaugh here, I shall be off and recommending myself to the others as well." He headed in the direction of Miss Tanning without a backward glance.

She closed her mouth. "He's rather, abrupt." She watched his back.

"Yes, he seems to be," Mr. Cavanaugh said.

They both watched Lord Bolton beeline it straight for Miss Tanning. "Hmm. And now we see, perhaps, the reason?" Mr. Cavanaugh rubbed his chin. "I hope you aren't too disappointed?"

In truth, something bothered her about his treatment, his quick dismissal and his obvious interest elsewhere. She couldn't account for her feelings, but she could dissuade Mr. Cavanaugh from his continued misunderstanding. "No, please. I have only the best wishes for Lord Bolton. I was just startled by his sudden entrance and have no further interest beyond that, I assure you."

His eyebrow rose. "Excellent. Then, shall we continue our walk?"

In truth, she could never understand this fascination with promenading about a smallish sort of room, but she forbore and was

19

grateful in the end to have met so many at the party. And doubly glad, for at the end, he returned her to the side of Lord Ridgecrest, who seemed pleased to have her company. She turned all attention to him, trying to ignore the overly exuberant Lord Bolton who was also at her side.

CHAPTER 3

*C*onfound it. *Lady* Felicity was she? A lady? And beautiful at that. And delightfully fun to tease. She stood in their small group at his side, with her back decidedly to him. Which he was perfectly agreeable to, because it isolated him and Miss Tanning a sufficient amount so as to give him a moment of privacy with her.

"Miss Tanning. You look well. The past weeks have been agreeable, I gather?"

"Yes, quite. We've been staying with friends here in Brighton, the Huntingtons. You might know them."

"Yes, good people. I was happy to hear of your attendance at this house party. I may not have come were it not for that pleasant discovery . . ."

"Oh, come now, Lord Bolton. We know you would have found merriment here regardless."

"Merriment and the sincerity of an attachment are two different things, my dear, and I was searching for an attachment." He stepped closer, allowing her to see the sincerity in his eyes. He was sincere, certainly, captivated by his goals. And would have been by her, he argued with himself, were he free to be captivated by just anyone of his acquaintance.

Lady Felicity's laugh tickled his consciousness with a curiosity about how he would go about bringing such a beautiful noise back to the surface of her primly proper expressions.

Miss Tanning shook her head. "You are too bold, which gives me leave to doubt your sincerity."

He reached for her hand, bowing. "Then, please, give me leave to prove my devotion. I am here only to win your goodwill."

Her eyes widened, and she looked around before returning her gaze to him. A slight pink colored her cheeks. "We shall see, then."

His nod made her smile. "The way I see it, you beautiful ladies may spend your time with any number of people, but if you are at liberty to choose, then why not pick those most amiable, those who can promise a closeness of relationship, an ease of living, generous and comfortable seasons in London, and an attentive partner. Who listens to your every whim?" He held her gaze and brought her hand again to his lips. "If you are able to choose, why not choose such a man?"

Their gaze was broken by Lord Ridgecrest. "Come, Bolton. Converse with us all."

He nodded to Miss Tanning and shifted his stance. Lord Ridge-crest broadened their circle so that he stood beside Miss Tanning and soon engrossed her in conversation.

Lady Felicity had shifted as well, closer to him. Seeing they would not be overheard, Abraham leaned nearer to her. "Lady Felicity?"

Her raised eyebrows made him laugh.

"I had no idea I was in such esteemed company when I imposed upon your kindness."

"Oh fiddle. I'm no more esteemed than the next lady. But I will say, I'm surprised to see you here."

"So, you did not know you were in such esteemed company either?"

Her face colored again, and he almost heard her laugh. He watched her choke it back. Such a pity for the sound was as delightful as it was contagious. "No, I had no way of even presuming such a thing."

"Ho, so you cut me to the core."

Their faces were close, surprisingly so, his impression of her being of the utmost propriety-following miss.

But she whispered, and he found her soft breath on his cheek captivating. "I heard what you said to Miss Tanning. Can you be serious?"

"Pardon me, Lady Felicity, but can you have been eavesdropping?"

She stepped back, "No!" Her voice carried to all nearby, enough for Lord Ridgecrest and Miss Tanning to halt in their discussion.

"What is it?" Lord Ridgecrest frowned at Lord Bolton, who held up his hands. "I cannot account for it, but that my retelling of a fascinating little tidbit from this past season has surprised our Lady Felicity."

Miss Tanning's eyes grinned in mischief at him. "Do tell us then.

We want to be a part."

"Well, I—" He glanced helplessly at Lady Felicity.

"It is all rather diverting. You'll soon join me in laughter, I'm certain."

"Yes, quite." An awkward pause followed, and Lady Felicity's eyes widened at him.

Then she cleared her throat. "I believe Lord Bolton is a bit embarrassed, so I shall share the story." She swallowed. "Of the two Miss Whites."

"The two Miss Whites?" Lord Bolton snorted.

"Well. Your story must have a name."

Lord Bolton bowed his head. "Quite right. Do carry on."

"He had promised a dance with Miss White. And all he knew of the woman was her hair was a honey gold and that she was about so high." She indicated a height much shorter than herself. "When it came time to fetch the woman, he went searching for a Miss White but found himself frustrated, for there are a significant number of women in a ballroom of honey-gold hair and that particular height."

"There are indeed." Miss Tanning stepped closer.

"But as he passed a group, he heard one of the men address just such a woman as Miss White."

"And there you have it." Mr. Cavanaugh clapped.

"Just so. He held out his arm and escorted the woman to the center of the floor and took his dance with her." She held up a finger. "Only to discover the lady's extreme discomfort in his great affront, for they had never been introduced."

Miss Tanning held a hand to her mouth. "No."

Lady Felicity dipped her head. "'Tis so. For not only are there many women of that description in a London ballroom, but apparently, more than one Miss White."

Their small group laughed. And Lord Bolton found himself once again highly amused at the plucky, though proper, Lady Felicity.

The footman announced, "A Mr. Garvey, Mrs. Garvey."

"Well. If it isn't our host himself." Mr. Cavanaugh coughed. "Miracles."

Mr. Garvey cleared his throat. "We are happy you have come. Please make yourselves comfortable and let our staff know if you are lacking in anything at all during your stay."

Mrs. Garvey shook her head. "Perhaps some things might be lacking. As no estate has every little necessity. But yes, welcome. We expect you will find great pleasure outside of the house, more so than in, I dare say. For example, we would like to invite you to choose from our stables a mount, and we will ride down by the water this evening after a quick supper. No need to waste daylight eating, not when there are sunsets to behold. We expect our party to be complete in number within the next few days."

The guests nodded their heads, and the few closest to the Garveys approached, conversing. Abraham grinned. "Miss Tanning. Are you seeking a riding partner for this evening?"

"I welcome company from all, naturally, but Lord Ridgecrest has asked me to be his particular partner." The smile she gave Ridgecrest was not lost on Abraham nor on Lady Felicity, apparently. Her body shook from what might have been a foot stomping. Curious. And diverting. His new prim friend had a surprising amount of emotion inside.

"In that case, Lady Felicity, would you be so kind as to join me?"

"Of course. Thank you."

"You can both join *us*. We'll all go together, I'd imagine." Lord Ridgecrest smiled at Lady Felicity, and Abraham wondered at their connection.

"Thank you." Her small smile she gifted Lord Ridgecrest seemed so different, so subservient compared to the woman he imagined tormented her prim and proper ways to no end.

Abraham had secured a place beside Miss Tanning at dinner. But the meal was not to be enjoyed. What could their hostess have been thinking, serving such a watered-down fare? Most guests finished unaccountably early and stood. He held his arm out for Miss Tanning to take. "I cannot understand the insolence of serving such a meal to guests." His mother would have been appalled. He remembered tears of regret over less than fine ingredients when they had started to run out of money. Her table, the food they presented to their guests, had always been a matter of personal pride with her. He couldn't decide if he should be insulted or disgusted with the Garveys. Or perhaps he should pity them.

"Oh, don't pay it any mind. Those of us who come often are not at all surprised. Wait until Mr. Garvey is present for a meal." She placed a hand on his arm and looked around at the other guests.

He decided not to dwell further on unpleasant topics. "I admit to a great amount of pleasure that the four of us will be riding together."

She nodded, a small smile on her lips. "Shall I see you at the stables, then?"

He bowed. "I shall be awaiting the moment."

She lifted her hand from his own and ascended the stairs with a certain grace he found appealing. It settled his irritation from dinner to see the manner in which she carried herself. Such poise, surely Miss Tanning would be an excellent addition to his estate. At last he turned from her and almost stumbled over Lady Felicity, who stood at his side with hands on her hips.

He jumped. "Why, Lady Felicity. What a wonderful surprise to see you sneaking up on me like that."

She frowned. "As if I would ever do such a thing. I simply waited until you were finished gawking and falling over yourself to please her."

"And what if I tell you I've noticed the same of you and Lord Ridgecrest?" He waved his hands at the lord's name.

"Then you would be as ridiculous as I already suspect you are."

He dipped his head. "I stand condemned. As ridiculous as you suspect I am." He turned from her. "Shall we meet at the stables to prove ourselves even more so to the others?"

She huffed. "I was only trying to help."

He waited.

"Yes. I'll be there straight away."

He turned from her down the opposite corridor. Why would she think of him as ridiculous? What was ridiculous? Was he not simply attempting to win Miss Tanning's hand? Was he behaving in a manner untoward? Confound Lady Felicity, he was all in a muddle about things now.

And she herself, swooning with raptures over Lord Ridgecrest. What a pair they made.

CHAPTER 4

Felicity's mare eased along the paths at the top of the cliffs. The wind whipped through her hair. Her bonnet had already lost its place on her head and hung, flinging itself about on her back. Her pins had all come loose, and much to her embarrassment, her hair flew out behind her, long and wild. The conditions were harsh, but the view . . . the view was unmatched in wild beauty. The ocean rose up in furious white caps, large waves reaching for a cloudy gray sky.

Miss Tanning's hair remained tightly wound at the back of her head. Her riding habit looked newer. Her boots shinier. No wonder the men all flocked to her. She looked the part. She seemed to have other facets of her personality to recommend her. She laughed easily. She was fun. By comparison, Felicity felt lacking.

Felicity rode alone while the two men fought for position at Miss Tanning's side. Only when the path became too narrow did one or the other come to ride beside her. Could she blame them? She looked a complete hoyden, hair coming more lose by the moment, a prime example of her mother's family. If the ride had not been so stunning, she would have wanted to return in complete mortification to Mrs. Dotting.

But she couldn't feel disheartened, not when the blue stretched to the edge of the world.

Lord Ridgecrest joined her. "I'm reminded of Dover and our time spent there."

She looked at the others, to see if they would hear.

"Conversation is nearly impossible unless we are close. They won't hear."

"Then you and I are in agreement that some things need not be discussed."

He nodded. "Although I don't regret the memories. Your mother, your family . . ." His eyes turned wistful, and Felicity found a lump in her throat. He inched closer, their legs almost touching as their mounts meandered on the path side by side. "I would be remiss if I did not express my utmost gratitude." His eyes were full of sincerity, his attention on her.

"I'm sure my mother would assure you your gratitude is not necessary. She would do the same tomorrow."

He nodded. "Seeing you again, and you, riding like this, with your hair all behind you. It's a sight I won't soon forget. You have much of your mother in you."

The way he said it made her proud of her mother, pleased to be a reminder of the beautiful woman. "Thank you. She was the best of women."

"I've rarely met someone of her character."

She rode higher in her saddle, the words of praise washing over. So often she'd heard nothing but scorn from anyone of title. "Such a boon to find someone from my past here. I feel as though you and I are close already because of it."

He cleared his throat and looked away.

Lord Bolton glanced back over his shoulder at her and then slowed his pace so that he rode between her and Lord Ridgecrest. "I've heard there's a run on candles at the house. Perhaps we should get back?"

Lord Ridgecrest hurried forward to take his former place beside Miss Tanning.

And Felicity could do nothing but frown at Lord Bolton.

"Ho, ho. Did I interrupt something important?" His eyes sparkled at her, and the more pleased and jovial he looked, the more irritated she became.

But then he rode even closer than Lord Ridgecrest had, leaned over to her and said, "I think we can help each other."

"Oh? In what manner?"

"Your conversation with Lord Ridgecrest just now. You're scaring him away."

She sucked in a breath. "Did you hear us?"

"Are you sharing secrets?"

Too close to the truth, she eyed him in suspicion and fear. What could he mean becoming involved in the past she would like to keep covered? "Not at all. I just don't see how my conversations with another . . ."

"Oh, come now, don't be missish. Listen while we have a moment."

She opened her mouth in shock. Was he now to include her in another outlandish scheme?

"You must allow *him* to pursue *you*, without such open provocation."

"What are you—"

"You were all too eager in the front room earlier, and just now, your comment about being close." He shivered. "That makes even me cringe."

She wished to turn away, but she had nowhere to turn.

"Look at you. Every man's dream of beauty, riding without societal constraints, your magnificent hair. You'd give every governess a heart attack and start every man's blood to boiling."

"I'm sure I don't—"

"He mentioned it, didn't he?"

She stopped and realized he had, but it was not at all what Lord Bolton was thinking. She shook her head.

"He did. You can't deny it." He held up a finger. "And then you ruined it with your closeness comment."

Had she? Tears burned in her eyes. Lord Bolton was too bold. She turned her head.

"I can help you win him."

She jerked her face back up to his.

"Absolutely. If you help me to do the same."

"But what can I possibly do to help you?" Hope rose within her. Lord Bolton seemed so sure.

31

"I'll tell you what to do when the time is right. You help me. I'll help you, and by the end of this party, both of us will leave with what we most desire right now." His eyes warmed as his gaze traveled over her face. And for a moment she questioned what she wanted most.

But then Miss Tanning's delighted laugh carried over on the wind to her, and she pressed her lips together. "Agreed."

Lord Bolton nodded a smile of victory. "The first thing to do, when we arrive at the stables, wait for Lord Ridgecrest to help you down off your horse."

"Shouldn't you do such a thing?"

"Well, normally I would be delighted to help you, except that I will be helping Miss Tanning. Let him help you. You'll see." His eyes sparkled with mischief, and she grinned in response without thinking. "And ask him about his horses." Then he clucked his tongue, and his horse sped up again.

Lord Ridgecrest returned to her side, and she remembered Lord Bolton's warning and advice. "You sit so well on your mount. Do you often ride?"

"Whenever I can. I shall attempt to ride in this very spot every day we are here." He looked out over the view of the land behind them. The hazy mist that hung over the water did not rise up to the land around her. The green of the grass, the craggy rocks, the rolling hills that continued out away from the ocean were really quite beautiful. She'd spent so much time studying Lord Ridgecrest, she'd hardly noticed.

When he turned his face back to her, she asked, "Do you have a fine stable?"

He carried on about his stallion, his mares, his home, and she listened, watching his face light up with excitement. A few more questions, and his conversation carried them all the way back to the stables on stories from home. By then, she felt she knew the personalities of the horses in half his stables.

"I bet you miss Thunder. Will you have your stallion at all during the party?"

The disappointment that clouded his eyes was charming. This man was very dedicated to his horses. "No. I had to leave him at my estate. But I'll be traveling there shortly after."

They approached the pastures behind the house on the Garvey estate. Smooth, cleared land spread out in front of her, and suddenly, she just wanted to ride out across it. She kicked her heels, and her horse jumped forward in a beautiful, smooth gallop. Laughing, her hands out at her sides, she tipped her had back and enjoyed the flying sensation of the horse beneath her.

A man's laughter surprised her at her side. Lord Bolton's face, grinning and bold, and Lord Ridgecrest's determined and focused on the other side. Was he trying to race? Of all the ridiculous…She leaned forward. He did the same. Lord Ridgecrest was determined to best her to the stables? Not today. Something about his face, his determined stance made her all the more anxious to win. She leaned forward, urging her horse.

Lord Ridgecrest did the same.

Lord Bolton sped up beside her, his face amused, but he shook his head.

Shook his head? He can't be shaking his head at her. She would dig deeper, beat him as well as Lord Ridgecrest.

The horse vibrated beneath her, muscles flexing and stretching in a beautiful synergy of motion. The stables were just at the top of the next hill, and she craved a victory. Her horse sped up, beating the others. Racing ahead, she crested the hill and tore into the paddock, beating everyone by a full horse breadth. They all turned and walked their horses while Miss Tanning approached.

"I'm quite diverted." She sat primly on her mount, back straight, riding habit precisely fitting, hair still neatly pinned under her bonnet.

Felicity puffed a strand of hair out of her face while she circled around the coral with her horse, walking her down. She knew she must look a sight. Deep embarrassment started to tighten up her insides, and at the moment all she wanted to do was run and hide. Lord Ridgecrest wouldn't look at her, his face suddenly stern, displeased.

Miss Tanning eyed her in amusement. Only Lord Bolton seemed as charming as ever. He rode up beside her. "I'm all amazement. Good win, my lady." He dipped his head.

But she turned away.

"Come now. We must be a good sport about our wins."

"Stop mocking me." Her words ended in a cry, and she blinked back her mortification.

He pulled up beside her. "Get a hold of yourself. Yes, you beat him in a horse race. Yes, he is fuming about it, but don't underestimate the attractiveness of your current state."

"My attractiveness?" She daren't even attempt a hand on her tresses to untangle them. What utter nonsense.

"Certainly. Your hair, your flushed cheeks. The daring sparkle in your eye, the aura of victory humming about you in the air. A man wouldn't be a man if he didn't notice." His eyes traveled her face, and she felt their path in a warmth across her skin. And for the first time in all her years, she felt desirable and wanted, for being herself. It wasn't the proper miss who was attractive to this man, but the part inside she so carefully tried to hide.

"Now." He leaned close, his whisper making her body hum with awareness. His eyes were daring, handsome; his hair, mussed from the wind, invited her fingers to toy with the wavy mass. Her cheeks burned as the realization of her thoughts hit her full force.

He murmured, "you must let him get you down off your horse."

She glanced at the stony-faced Lord Ridgecrest. "I don't think—"

"Trust me."

She swallowed. Then nodded. "But if he doesn't help me, you must come and do so yourself. I'll not be left here by myself . . ."

"Of course. But he will." Lord Bolton winked and rode over to the stable hand waiting to take his horse.

Felicity circled two times more while Miss Tanning dismounted, Lord Bolton holding her about the waist.

Felicity's cheeks burned anew, watching his hands at Miss Tanning's side. And now she understood. She waited for Lord Ridgecrest to dismount first, but he stalled, and she stalled, and Lord Bolton was deep in conversation with Miss Tanning, the two of them still standing very close together. Something about their moment and Lord Ridgecrest's delay burned frustration within her. She kicked up her heels and slid to a stop in front of them, waiting with raised eyebrows.

Lord Ridgecrest called from behind. "Allow me, my lady."

Lord Bolton winked and then led Miss Tanning away.

The staff took care of Lord Ridgecrest's horse, and then Felicity held her breath as he approached from behind. "That's so kind of you."

He appeared in front of her and waited below her, unmoving as of yet. She couldn't read his expression, so she was unsure what to do or say as she stared down from her horse. Was this one of those moments when eyes met and hearts pounded? The nervous flutterings of her own heart were a strong indication she was affected by him. Was his own heart behaving normally? How could one tell?

At last he reached his hands up, and the pressure at her waist thrilled her. But as she slid down, breathtakingly close to Lord Ridgecrest, it was Lord Bolton's wink that replayed itself through her mind. Lord Ridgecrest eyed her and then shook his head, a small smile playing at his lips. "You've bested me today. I don't often experience that from a woman."

Shame filled her before a spark of indignation arose inside. Still, she dipped her head. "Should I apologize? I promise I'm way more behaved, usually, quite the napoleon to my own chaperone."

"Napoleon." He shook his head. "Apologies totally unnecessary." He lifted her chin with his finger. "I don't mind being bested by one so lovely." His eyes traveled over her hair. And for the second time this late afternoon, she felt beautiful.

"Thank you. I have a bit of a competitive nature. I've tried to stamp it out . . ."

"I'm sure with a few more seasons, you'll see more of the way of things."

Her breath shuddered. "A few more. . ."

"But I'm happy I was gifted to see this side of you. To remember

36

from whence you've come." He stepped back. "And to give you my thanks."

She took the arm he offered and walked back through the stables in silence. He stopped to greet a few of the horses.

"Fine horseflesh, this. Old Mr. Garvey has a beautiful collection."

Their host walked in the door. "I'm happy you were able to enjoy some of my mounts. Tell me, was it to your satisfaction?"

"Excellent ride, and countryside. I dare say Brighton boasts some of the most beautiful views England has to offer."

"That it does." They made their way out of the stables, and the men fell in step with one another. Mr. Garvey rubbed his chin. "I hear you are in the market for another mare."

The resulting conversation gifted Felicity with some quiet moments to her own thoughts. What had she done? Had Lord Ridgecrest just dismissed the thought of an alliance with her? Perhaps. And standing so close to him, his hands at her waist, was oddly flat feeling. The thrill she'd felt at imagining Lord Bolton's hands at her waist was an entirely different experience. She sucked in a breath. "No."

No, no, no, no, no. I am not attracted to that lord.

She walked closer to hear more of the conversation between Lord Ridgecrest and Mr. Garvey, but no matter what she did, thoughts of Lord Bolton returned.

CHAPTER 5

"Keep your eye on the prize, man." Abraham lifted his chin for the valet, who was obviously so used to his random mumblings that he didn't even answer. "She is nothing to you."

But even after a fitful sleep, he could not forget Lady Felicity, eyes alight with joy, hair streaming out behind her in a beautiful wave. She was absolutely the most stunning woman Abraham had ever seen. He shook his head, the valet pausing in his tying of the cravat. Abraham had best remember that Lady Felicity was not Miss Tanning.

And Miss Tanning's eyes had lit when he lowered her from her horse. Miss Tanning had agreed to a walk this morning, and Miss Tanning had twenty thousand pounds to her name. He'd never even heard of Lady Felicity before now. He guessed she came from an obsolete, small estate—her father was perhaps a baron. Abraham considered her in a different light. Perhaps he would ask Ridgecrest. The man seemed to know her previously.

No matter what Lady Felicity turned out to be, he was making progress with Miss Tanning, and he could not afford to lose ground there. He considered his bargain with Lady Felicity. He'd seek her out today. She was going about her pursuit of Lord Ridgecrest all wrong, though if the man didn't see what a stunning creature she was, he was daft and blind. And couldn't be helped. Abraham snorted. She'd beat the man who prized horseflesh and his seat above all else, beat him on a horse. Ridgecrest wouldn't heal his hurt pride for days, Abraham was certain of it. The memory was assuredly burned into his soul. And not for the same reasons, Abraham was having a difficult time forgetting the ride.

Simmons cleared his throat.

"What is it?"

"Mr. Garvey has left again this morning."

"Odd host, to leave his own party."

"They say he is invited to events with Prince George." Simmons straightened Abraham's jacket. "Cook has warned us all, breakfast will be a light fare."

Abraham snorted. "If it's anything like our supper, I might choose to eat elsewhere."

"I know a few of the guests have done precisely that. There is a bakery in town that boasts an assortment that might tempt your eye."

"Thank you, Simmons. You are a gem. I shall bring you back something."

He nodded. "I would not complain. Thank you, my lord."

"I suspect you suggested it because you were worried about your own meal as much as mine?"

He grunted.

Abraham smiled. "We shan't be here forever Simmons. Try to forbear."

Abraham made his way downstairs, determined to spend the entire day convincing Miss Tanning to accept his suit. Thanks to his valet, he knew precisely where their morning walk should take them. The bake shop.

He did not even enter the parlor where breakfast awaited on the sideboard, but waited in the front foyer by the door. The home was finely appointed. The magnificent stairwell rising up behind him would impress any visitor.

Movement caught his eye coming from one of the hallways that fed into this main entryway. A brightly colored skirt stepped back again into the shadows. Curious. He waited. And then she came into view again, a nonchalant façade firmly in place. Lady Felicity. She walked by him as if to pretend he wasn't there, her small nose in the air while she studied the paintings on the opposite wall and then the stairwell. She spent an inordinate amount of time studying the staircase. Was she planning to ignore him altogether? His smile grew. And he cleared his throat.

She stopped. "Oh. Lord Bolton. Hello." Her overly large surprise at happening upon him made him grin. What was she about?

"Are you going in to breakfast?"

She wrinkled her nose. "No, I was up early and tasted a few bites. That was sufficient."

He stepped closer. "We have not as yet had the chance to converse about the results of your efforts yesterday. Lord Ridgecrest helped you down from your horse?"

She blushed furiously, and the disappointment that niggled at his amusement surprised him. Did he wish she would blush in reaction to his own efforts?

She found her voice. "He did."

"And?"

She shrugged, her shoulder lifting in one delicate rise. "And we will see, won't we?"

Chattering voices sounded from the breakfast room, and Abraham recognized Miss Tanning. "And now I could use a bit more of your assistance."

Then Miss Tittering's nasal sounds joined that of Miss Tanning.

"Oh bother."

Lady Felicity's eyes widened. "Is that?"

"The woman on the beach."

"She thinks I'm someone's ward, a Miss Bumbly."

"And Miss Tanning knows you for you."

She widened her eyes in panic. "What shall we do?" Then her lips pursed, and she crossed her arms. "I should very well let you try and talk your way around this mishap, since it is your doing."

"Perhaps it best you hide?"

"For the entire house party?"

"No, of course not, but at least in this moment until we can contrive a solution?" The sound of chattering had paused at the door, but any moment, the women could walk through. His eyes pleaded with her. What an odd turn of events that he should so desperately need this woman's assistance on multiple occasions.

"Oh, very well." She hurried down the hallway from whence she came just as he turned to greet the women. She called over her shoulder. "But this must be addressed, before dinner and parlor games."

"What a pleasant happenstance." He smiled and then bowed in greeting to Miss Tanning, Miss Tittering, Mrs. Harrow, and two other women to whom he had not yet been introduced.

Miss Tanning offered her hand, which he took and placed a kiss upon. She turned to the others. "We have all have expressed a desire to walk this morning, perhaps as far as town?"

Abraham swallowed back his immense disappointment at sharing Miss Tanning's company. Did he imagine it, or was Lady Felicity's giggle moving down the hallway behind him? Oh, she would enjoy his torment. "I would be delighted. Shall we begin?" He held his arm for Miss Tanning to take, and then Miss Tittering stood on his other side, clutching at his arm. Soon he was overwhelmed with womanly chatter.

Miss Tittering was still chattering on after they'd walked to the end of the drive and down the path that would lead them to a row of shops and stores on this side of Brighton. "And I just couldn't believe my luck to happen upon our dear Lord Bolton on the beach just yesterday."

He nodded. Miss Tanning had given up pretending interest and was focused on the beautiful views out to their right. The rocky cliff edge behind them, the water to their side, and the lovely tall grasses and windy path to their front. Abraham would have been enchanted, had he the good fortune of Miss Tanning by herself, or at least more closed-lipped company.

"You won't believe it. But he was escorting someone's ward, and I thought to myself, what a dear man."

He cleared his throat.

"Who but the most caring among us would do such a thing, and at a house party no less."

"Well, actually—"

"I saw her. She's here at the party with us, if you can believe it. And living in excellent circumstances if what I'm hearing is correct."

Excellent circumstances? He waited for Miss Tittering to continue, but she did not. Blast the woman, in the one second her chatter had at last become interesting, she became fixated on something in her reticule.

"I do feel it incumbent upon me to explain her situation. I have since learned her to be titled, and perhaps not the ward I once thought?"

Miss Tanning raised both eyebrows. "Not the ward you once thought?"

"No, it's all very interesting and surprising really, but she's here with us and a good friend of Lord Ridgecrest. Miss Tanning knows her as well. Lady Felicity."

Her confusion warred across her face, and Abraham didn't know what else to do but spell it out straight.

Miss Tittering had at last sorted through her reticule, and Abraham knew she was about to begin again so he said, "Miss Tanning, tell us of your home."

Her face softened. "It is the best of places. I know of no other location in all of England half so lovely as the rolling hills of the Lake District."

"Oh, then you feel right at home near the ocean." Abraham wished to rest a hand over her own, but with his arm otherwise engaged, he tried to feel satisfied with their limited closeness.

She continued on about her family, her father's employment as the local clergy, her stables at home, and he found his mind wandering. Lady Felicity's race to the stables, her head leaning forward, eyes full of fire, was never far from his mind. He snorted back a laugh.

"Did I say something funny?" Miss Tanning's disapproving expression chastised his woolgathering.

"No, certainly not."

"I would think the loss of our dear mare would not be at all amusing."

"I do apologize. Sometimes when our emotions are strongest, they appear the most disheveled. I most certainly did not wish to laugh at such a loss. Tell me more about her."

She seemed somewhat mollified, but he took care to pay close attention and did enjoy a dimple that made an appearance now and then. He enjoyed her quiet nature and her intelligence, and the longer he eased into the slow movement of her quips and tales of home, the more he admitted that life with her could be nice, slow, good.

They at last made it to the street, and the other two who had been walking behind them gathered around. "They are said to have a good assortment of ribbons."

"I am at your leisure. We can go into every shop, but we must pay a visit to the bake shop."

"Oh yes. Let's go there first."

The group as one entered the shop to a very pleased shopowner. "Do I have the pleasure of serving more of the Garveys' guests?"

Abraham nodded. "You most certainly do."

They gathered at a table with their choice of items from the bakery. He got a couple custards and something that made him grin, a Banbury cake. "Do you know the meaning of these lovely pastries?" He held up a bit with his fork. "Banbury cakes."

"That's a Banbury cake? As in, to tell a Banbury?"

The other ladies gasped at Miss Tittering's crass comment.

"It is a rather uncouth word, is it not? But my dear ladies, it comes from so simple a thing as this innocuous treat right here." He offered a bite to Miss Tanning. She dipped her head in a deep blush but then lifted her chin and accepted a piece from him.

As he watched her lips close around the currant-filled pastry, he expected to feel some sense of excitement at so intimate a gesture, but instead, he felt rather flat. A wave of disappointment hit him. He knew he'd be marrying someone for her assets, but the romantic part of his sensibilities had hoped that more might develop, at least a bit of heart thumping. But that hadn't happened since the last time he'd been with Lady Felicity.

CHAPTER 6

Felicity and Mrs. Dotting set out to find the drawing room. Lord Ridgecrest was nowhere to be seen, and she knew some of the group had set out for the bake shop in town shortly after Lord Bolton had left. She approached one of the maids. "Would you mind telling me where I might find a group of the ladies?"

The bright young girl smiled and curtseyed. "Yes'm. M'lady. There are a group of them taking tea in the conservatory."

The ladies had a table and chairs set up with beautiful lace and tea but few cakes, fewer sandwiches. Felicity remembered some of their names.

Mrs. Daw met her at the glass door that led into the conservatory. The housekeeper was a cheery woman with eyes that sparkled like Felicity's grandmother's. "Oh, Mrs. Daw. How are you this morning?"

"I'm well, m'dear. I wish I had a few more sweet things for your tea, but it is lovely here, isn't it?"

"It's completely charming."

The worried expression cleared, and her eyes shone with a pleased expectation. "It is charming, isn't it? That lace comes from the missus's great-grandmother."

"Does it really?" Felicity stepped into the group of ladies and fingered it. "I've never been good at tatting, especially not this quality. The stitch work is also remarkable."

Miss Tinsdale, a lovely but quiet woman she'd met yesterday, patted the chair beside her. "Do sit and join us, Lady Felicity, Mrs. Dotting."

"I'd be delighted. I came to find you and was pleased to see you situated in such a pleasant circumstance." She turned to Mrs. Daw. "You could stay and join us . . ."

"I should say not." Miss Hastings's eyebrows were so far up in her hairline, Felicity wondered if they had been lost.

Mrs. Daw chuckled. "Now, that wouldn't be right, would it? But I'll tell you ladies a secret I don't tell every guest."

They leaned forward, even Miss Hastings, who had found the idea of associating with Mrs. Daw so abhorrent moments before.

"I keep tarts in the kitchen. If you find yourself not being able to sleep, I'm often in there finishing up a batch. I'd welcome a bit of company any time." She patted Felicity on the shoulder, and the motherly nature of the gesture nearly brought tears to Felicity's eyes.

"Thank you, Mrs. Daw. I might join you this very evening, then."

"I'd be pleased." She nodded and then left them to the maids and footman.

Miss Hastings took the liberty of pouring tea. "I'm afraid it's rather weak."

"Like every meal we've had."

Felicity smiled, shaking her head. She'd never been to a house party before, but surely they were not all like this one. She sipped and tried not to make a face. "Their conservatory is lovely. At least there's that."

Miss Tinsdale smiled gratefully. "I am looking forward to exploring. I hear they have a particularly rare lemon tree. And some species of rose that their gardeners are creating right now."

Felicity could tell she was holding back a measure of her exuberance. So, Miss Tinsdale was a horticulturist. How interesting. Felicity had a new interest in talking with her. "Perhaps we could walk together and you could point out different species of interest?"

Miss Hastings snorted, but Miss Larkin, a previously quiet young lady piped up, "Oh, I would enjoy that as well."

"Then it is decided." Felicity stood. "Shall we? Unless you are enjoying your tea?"

They all stood, even Miss Hastings. Miss Larkin led the way with Mrs. Dotting at her side.

To Felicity's surprise, Miss Hastings sidled up next to her, placing a hand on her arm. "I think we can become friends. Though I do not hold a title myself, most of my friends are from the highest, most impeccable families."

Felicity swallowed. A sudden, unexpected thrill at being thought of in such a manner felt delicious. She imagined for a moment that she was entering Almack's, that eyes turned to her with hopeful expectation. Men lined up to fill her dance schedule. And no one looked away with raised eyebrows. The comfortable feelings of acceptance washed through her. But then she remembered all those years of women such as Miss Hastings, sidling up with others, looking over their shoulders in superiority. So she said only, "I'd like to know you better, Miss Hastings. Thank you for the distinction in singling me out."

"Oh, well certainly. And we cannot deny the interest from one male gentleman." Her eyes sparkled with the enticement of new secrets.

"Has there been such a one? I'm afraid I'm unaware." She tried to stem the hope that rose inside. Could it be Lord Ridgecrest was interested enough that others, too, were noticing?

Miss Hastings whispered. "Certainly, Lord Bolton is not one to be overlooked. As handsome as he is." She giggled, and Miss Tinsdale looked over her shoulder from their front, an all too familiar, self-conscious expression tightening her face. Irritation rose fast and furiously in Felicity. "Lord Bolton indeed." She called up to Miss Tinsdale. "Come now, let us discuss the flora. Miss Tinsdale, I am most anxious to learn about the chocolate tree I hear might be growing here."

The exclamations of curiosity and new energy in the group made Felicity smile. But she didn't miss the narrowed eyes of Miss Hastings. As Felicity hurried forward to join the others, she pressed her hand on the miss's arm. "My apologies. I've realized we are neglecting our tour guide. But you should know, my interests lie elsewhere, and I assure you, his do as well."

Miss Hastings pressed her lips together. "So you say." Her eyebrow rose. "But if you're certain you are uninterested, then he is a prize to be won for any of us, is he not? Penniless though he is, at least his face and amiability recommend him."

Penniless? She did not know much about Lord Bolton. She dipped her head and hurried forward to join the others gathered around a small, unassuming bit of green, just unfurling leaves from the dark rich soil.

Lord Bolton indeed. He'd ruin her chances if she wasn't careful, especially if people were already talking, noticing them together. She thought back on their hurried conversations, their secretive glances. The whole of the party guests, including Lord Ridgecrest, could easily have thought them to be forming an attachment. She bit back a groan. Well, no matter. She would now avoid Lord Bolton no matter what further emergencies or need for subterfuges would befall him. The thought gave her great satisfaction and only a hint of disappointment. For his jovial smile and his help in winning Lord Ridgecrest had been a useful and diverting distraction.

FELICITY HAD CONTINUED the tour of the conservatory with a properly concealed but raging compulsion to find Lord Bolton and expose him for the outrageous flirt that he was. If he ruined her last chance at a respectable marriage, she would never forgive him. She snorted. What good would that do? He would be unaffected by her.

She walked sedately at Mrs. Dotting's side, heading to the parlor for games, belying the silent fury that energized her thoughts. "You must assist me in avoiding Lord Bolton wherever possible. If he approaches, you must engage him in conversation while I escape."

"Really, do you feel such measures to be necessary?"

"I certainly do. People are talking." She calmed her breathing. "If possible, it would be better were I to never be near him again."

"Might prove difficult since we are all at the same house party."

She sighed. "And I would leave, were it not for our urgent need to . . ." She searched the area around them. "Secure the affections of another."

Mrs. Dotting dabbed her brow. "In that regard, I do feel you've had some success?"

"I do believe I have. If I can but continue to draw his eye . . ." The helpful tips already offered by Lord Bolton came to mind. She'd come to rely on his opinions too much in regards to capturing Lord Ridgecrest's attention.

"How could he not notice you? This new dress is lovely. One of your finest."

"Thank you." She shook the skirts, enjoying their responding shimmer. The light blue, almost white, trailed to the ground, a wide ribbon of deep pink tied at her waist. Her neckline was lined with the same coloring in lace and ribbon. "I think the pink aids in my complexion." Her mother had said so countless times. Thinking of her now brought such a tinge of sorrow, tears brimmed at her eyes. She turned away and blinked furiously, but one fell down her cheek.

"Oh, my lady, your eyes will be red. What is the matter?" Mrs. Dotting dug in her reticule for a handkerchief, but Lord Ridgecrest surprised them both with his appearance and offered one.

"May I?"

Felicity reached for the lovely white handkerchief and rested her hand on the arm he offered. "You've come to my rescue, my lord. Thank you." She allowed all of her pleased reaction to him to show on her face. But Lord Bolton's advice came to mind, and she bit back any overexuberant expressions that came to mind. Such as, *Your timing is so impeccable, I wonder if we are of one mind already.*

He dipped his head. "I'm happy to hear I can be of assistance."

She offered it back, and he shook his head. "You may keep it."

Her face heated, but she tucked it carefully away in her reticule, trying to appear less affected than she was. "Will you be playing whist? Or are you more of a hazard player?"

"I am not one for games usually, but I might be cajoled into it if a certain lovely lady were to request." He winked.

She sucked in her breath. "I will keep that in mind. I for one enjoy a good game, but I find other activities much more useful, more proper, as cards tends to bring out a competitive nature in the best of us, and one not so ladylike as perhaps you would expect."

He chuckled. "No fear of that side showing to me. We have no secrets between us."

Concerned, she added. "Though I don't feel the need to suppress any tendencies you may suspect from my childhood. One outgrows those rather completely."

He nodded absentmindedly as they approached the opened double doors. They were early, apparently, for few had arrived. "Where shall I leave you? It seems I have forgotten an item in my room."

"Oh, well. I would be happiest right over there in that chair with the needlepoint. A group of ladies and I are all hoping to work together and finish it by the end of the party, a gift for the Garveys."

He hardly heard, his glance checking the entrance enough times, she suspected whom he sought. "Very well. I'll leave you to it, then." He bowed and clicked his heels as he moved from the room.

Mrs. Dotting frowned. "Not sure what to make of that lord."

"Nor I, to tell you the truth. But come. We mustn't concern ourselves. He said he would return and that he could be convinced to play a game if I asked." She straightened her back in pleased success. "That has to mean something."

Mrs. Dotting sat at her side, lifting a book from a nearby table. "It appears you are correct, my lady." Her expression blank, Felicity could not read what she might be hiding, but she suspected Mrs. Dotting had thoughts she kept to herself.

"Who do you prefer?"

"Pardon me?"

"Of the two men we've come to know so far, who would you marry?"

Mrs. Dotting's mouth dropped open. "I'm sure I don't know how to answer that question."

Felicity watched her, but she lifted the book and said no more. So Felicity lifted her needle and began to add flowers to the design.

"Lord Bolton is just so jovial, kind, and pleasing to look upon, is he not?"

The book remained raised, and that's all Mrs. Dotting would say, but Felicity couldn't help but consider her words. Yes, he was jovial, kind . . . her heart sped up . . . And pleasing to look upon. But he was not well mannered. He was presumptuous. And . . .fixated on a singular course to win over Miss Tanning. She wondered at the disappointment that filled her. "I heard he is penniless."

"Well, that shouldn't signify to you, should it?"

"Not necessarily, but there is likely a reason for his impoverished state."

Mrs. Dotting grunted and turned a page.

Felicity eyed the room. A few of the ladies had gathered, taking up places about the room in relatively quiet pursuits. She smiled in satisfaction. As it should be. Two new women to whom Felicity had not yet been introduced were in conversation with one another on the other side of the room. Felicity immediately hoped they might be friends. They both looked up and smiled. "Who are they?"

Mrs. Dotting glanced over her shoulder. "Oh, that'd be the Lady Anslowe and Miss Lucy Brook. They both have interesting bits of gossip—"

"Gossip? Mrs. Dotting, are we to resort to the habits of small-minded creatures and share negative news about another?"

Mrs. Dotting puffed and prattled for a moment before she said, "I was only going to say what I've heard that's positive . . ." She turned another page and stayed silent.

Which Felicity found difficult to resist. "Oh, do tell it, then. I long for friends. Perhaps they might be the sort?"

"Well, the one on the right is an heiress. You can't tell by looking at her, I know, but she owns and runs, mind you, a bank."

Felicity eyed her with a new admiration. "But surely that's not respectable? For a woman?"

"There are some that might think as you, but I'm of the sort that thinks it's perfectly respectable for her to own a bank."

Felicity nodded. "Just so." But after so many years of some in society turning up their noses at her mother's family's source of income, she didn't quite know what to think about a woman boldly out in society as a bank owner.

Mrs. Dotting leaned closer. "Apparently, there's been some talk questioning the bank's stability with the likes of her in charge, but I'm of the mind to put more money in there. Just to show the world what I think of their opinions." She lifted her book again and Felicity laughed. "You, Mrs. Dotting are quiet liberally minded."

"I guess in this instance, I am."

Felicity considered Miss Brook. She seemed so unassuming, pretty, but nothing in her appearance led Felicity to believe she carried a certain powerful leadership that controlled men and their placement of money. She found herself a bit in awe of the woman. "And who's the other?"

"She and her husband have come to the party together." Lord and Lady Anslowe. She paused as if this information were heavy with meaning.

"And is that unexpected?"

"Oh, it most certainly is, because they haven't lived together yet. She lives in the north and he stays in London, from the moment of their marriage."

Felicity continued with her stitching, pondering the plight of others. Everyone's life situations were so different from one another. Perhaps there wasn't simply one standard by which to live, one set of rules dictated by the governesses. "We give those women a lot of power."

"Pardon me?" Mrs. Dotting looked around. "Who?"

"Our governesses."

"Power? Whatever do you mean by that?"

"Oh, never you mind. I'm suddenly questioning a few things, that is all. I'll probably return to normal by morning."

As she stitched, the more she wondered if perhaps her outlook on life, her perception of her own unworthiness, was taught to her by small-minded people. Here at the house party were women of all backgrounds, all circumstances. And each accepted in her way.

She found the space underneath her stitching and poked the needle up through the back just as a booming voice entered the room. "Come, Miss Tanning. We must be partners at whist."

Mrs. Dotting smiled over the top of her book, and Felicity groaned. "We must not notice Lord Bolton, Mrs. Dotting. Stop smiling. Stop . . . smiling."

"I shall gather our table full of players, Miss Tanning, never you fear."

"Is he coming?" Felicity hissed to Mrs. Dotting.

"I'm not looking."

A pair of Hussein's sat down beside her.

She lifted her eyes to a chagrined Lord Bolton.

"What, may I ask, are you doing? Lady Felicity, surely this cannot be."

"I don't understand." She shook unaccountably at his presence, so much so that she daren't lift the needle.

"Are you not still about the task of garnering attention from perfection in manhood himself, Lord Ridgecrest?"

She cleared her throat and looked around. Thankfully no one seemed to be hearing his words.

"Will you please speak quieter? Really, Lord Bolton. I hardly think it proper to discuss such a subject so openly."

"That is beside the point I'm trying to make, which is you had best desist in the art of needlework this instant and come play a game of whist."

"What? Why would I do that? We're working on a gift."

He peered over her shoulder. "That is quite lovely, I will admit. A gift for whom?" He reached a finger out, not touching the flowers she'd been working on but nearly. "And who did this bit right here? It is exquisite."

"Why, that was me. I did that while I waited for others to come."

"My mother and my grandmother would be impressed."

"I—what?"

"Yes, precisely. Needlepoint is for the purpose of impressing men's mothers in your training as a proper wife. It means nothing at all to the men in the room."

"You just pointed out . . ."

"Well, except perhaps to me. I do find that bit catching and would talk some more about it, but no other man is going to care about the precise smallness of your stitches." He held a hand out to escort her. "Come now, we must be about whist. We shall garner a partner for you, and then when the mysterious perfect man shows up, you will be engaging and fun and he will wish he were your partner."

She couldn't refuse. They'd already spent enough time talking in hushed tones. Everyone was bound to suspect what Miss Hastings had accused, that he was actively pursuing her. So she placed her hand in his. The thrilling warmth that filled her raced through her stomach, flipping it around in excited circles. "Oh."

His eyes darkened for a moment, and he narrowed the space between them. "Just so." Then he blinked, straightened, and led her over to the table where Miss Tanning was waiting.

Felicity realized as she sat and situated herself that she didn't even hope for Lord Ridgecrest to come. She was quite satisfied with things just as they were. And that was the most dangerous way for her to feel right now, when it was of highest urgency that she win over Lord Ridgecrest before he was convinced by any other female.

CHAPTER 7

*L*ord Bolton leaned forward and winked at Felicity and Miss Tanning. "And now we wait for our fourth."

Mr. Chamberlain approached at a nearby table. His four began to play at once. Miss Hastings glanced over her shoulder at the empty chair and raised her eyebrows at Lady Felicity before turning her superior expressions back toward Mr. Chamberlain.

And suddenly, Abraham wanted nothing more to do with Miss Hastings.

Miss Tanning fiddled with the cards. "Lady Felicity, do you play the piano forte?"

"I do. Yes. Do you?"

Her answer intrigued Abraham, for most ladies qualified the statement with their deplorable lack of skill or their willingness to play for others. Her simple answer made him immediately wish to hear her play. "Then we shall have to hear all you ladies play. Do you play Miss Tanning?"

"I do as well. My friends often request that I play for them. I don't know whether out of friendship alone or enjoyment of my talent." She lowered her lashes, and Abraham was amused at her typical debutante response. Either the ladies were not much to be celebrated by their own admission, or their friends thought highly of their musicality.

"I should like to hear you both, then, perhaps tomorrow after breakfast?"

"Perhaps." Lady Felicity watched the door.

Where was that dratted Ridgecrest?

"I could go and fetch our elusive fourth member, I suppose."

"No!" Miss Tanning and Lady Felicity exclaimed together.

Their cheeks equally pink, Abraham had to wonder at their reaction. Did Lady Felicity not wish to play whist with Lord Ridgecrest? And why should Miss Tanning care at all?

He shifted in his seat, suddenly uncomfortable. Lady Felicity would not meet his eyes, and Miss Tanning watched the entry doors an unnecessary amount. This would not do.

A gasp interrupted whatever Miss Tanning would have said next, for a shadow stood in the doorway. A man with broad shoulders, thick arms, a tanned face, and hair tied back behind him.

The footman announced. "Lord Bellingham."

Silence followed his announcement. All in the room rose and bowed or curtsied, and Lord Bellingham followed suit.

"Do you know who that is?" Miss Tanning leaned forward.

Miss Hastings, who sat at her left, said, "He's been in India. I wonder why he's suddenly returned . . ." She frowned. "And why he's here now."

His eyes seemed fierce, and he carried himself as though he were in pain. Before Abraham could stop himself, he waved the man over.

But Ridgecrest had chosen that moment to make an appearance as well. He bowed. "Might I have this spot?"

Lady Felicity nodded. "Yes, we are waiting on one more."

He sat just as Lord Bellingham arrived at their side.

Abraham stood again. "Have you just come to join us? I would like to make the introductions, but I am at a great disadvantage."

"I can do the honors." Lord Ridgecrest stood again. "For I just met him in the hallway. Lord Bolton, Lady Felicity, Miss Tanning, this is Lord Bellingham. I think we will find him an interesting conversationalist, for he's just returned from India."

"Oh have you?" Lady Felicity smiled at him in a manner she had no business sharing with other men. Abraham wanted to step in front of Lord Bellingham so as to feel some of the sunshine warmth of her smile on him instead. What an absurd thought.

Ridgecrest seemed impervious to the ladies' reactions or to the intrigue of the man towering over them.

Abraham nodded again. "We were just about to play whist. We'd enjoy an audience, Bellingham, if you'd care to join us. And Ridgecrest, your chair."

"Oh, of course." Lord Ridgecrest smiled at everyone in their group, his gaze lingering overly long on Miss Tanning, and Lord Bolton frowned. Perhaps he had missed something significant. Lady

Felicity seemed to notice as well, and her look of great discomfort and self-conscious embarrassment nudged Abraham's protective instincts. "Shall we begin?"

They passed out the cards. And Lord Bellingham excused himself to talk with someone on the opposite side of the room.

When Abraham returned his attention to the cards, Lord Ridgecrest and Miss Tanning were making eyes at one another, and Lady Felicity looked like she wished to disappear.

Abraham cleared his throat. "Lady Felicity, I hear, is excellent on the piano forte."

She raised her eyes in alarm and looked from Lord Ridgecrest to him and back. "I, um. Thank you." She shook her head at Lord Ridgecrest, only a fraction, but Abraham noticed and he couldn't for the life of him understand why such an innocuous comment would arouse concern. "She has agreed to play for us tomorrow after we breakfast. Perhaps you'd like to join us?" He watched Ridgecrest's hesitation with growing irritation. "Miss Tanning will also be joining us and favoring us with a number."

"Will she! I'd be delighted. Thank you for mentioning it so that I might also benefit."

As he watched Lady Felicity sink further into a shell, he sat up straighter and allowed her to see his cards.

Her eyes widened, then he winked and hid them. Her face reddened but just as he hoped. That tiny sparkle of competitive rebellion he'd noticed on the beach surfaced, and she placed a winning card.

Lord Ridgecrest sighed overly loud. "Not the best card to place at this moment, but I don't expect you to understand the subtlety of the game. I'll try and cover for us both."

Lady Felicity's eyes widened, but that's all the indication Abraham received of her emotion. Hopefully she was furious. Because Abraham would have been.

He and Miss Tanning placed their own cards, and Lady Felicity won, as they both knew she would.

She then won all the remaining hands to her growing delight. Abraham chuckled at her incredible competitive urges. Gathering all the cards to her, she glowed. "Would you like to play again?"

Lord Ridgecrest sniffed. "I believe it might be time to switch up the partners."

Her face fell. "Oh? I would think we make a good team."

"Perhaps in whist, but there are other reasons to team up, are there not?" He looked at Abraham and Miss Tanning. "Did you know Lady Felicity and I are formerly acquainted?"

She sucked in her breath.

"I did not know that." Abraham eyed Lady Felicity, but she refused to look at him. She refused to look anywhere but at Lord Ridgecrest. And his eyes were challenging and a bit unkind, if he were to guess.

"Yes. It is difficult to rise from our roots, or to move past embarrassment if one keeps company with those who know enough to keep us where we should never elevate past."

Lady Felicity's face went ashen, and Abraham thought she might faint. His ire rose further. He cleared his throat.

"I think just the opposite would be true. Anyone who knew me as a lad was sure to be forever tainted against me. But at the same time, they would hold a special regard as some of the few who can claim a more intimate knowledge of me and my life. A blessing and a curse, I suppose."

Lady Felicity turned grateful eyes to him, and their depths held his attention for many moments. Such a beautiful color. The blue actually had specks of yellow to give the impression of green in some lighting. And her upper cheeks had a smattering of freckles also, which he hadn't noticed before. Her cheeks held a hint of rose to them, and her upper lip curled in such a charming indent, he found his gaze tracing the line of her mouth.

Lord Ridgecrest shuffled the cards, the noise pulling Abraham away from such a fascinating perusal. But his sneer reminded Abraham of the reason for his comment.

Lady Felicity reached for the cards. "I think we should warn them about the birds."

Abraham opened his mouth in amazement. Then he bit his cheek to keep from laughing out right.

Her lips twitched with amusement. *Oh, good show, Lady Felicity.* "Excellent thought." He leaned forward and drew the attention of the other four. "There are some dangers on the beach to be aware of."

"Dangers?" Miss Hastings rested her cards face down to focus completely on him.

Lady Felicity nodded. "Most certainly. We witnessed one ourselves."

"You should explain, Lady Felicity, for I don't think I can do the story justice."

"Well, you see, we happened upon one another quite by accident before the party started."

"She saved me, outright."

"Well, I wouldn't go so far as to claim—"

"Do not be modest. I might have suffered tremendously were it not for you."

"Possibly a cut right to your eye, if not for me." She snorted. And then covered her mouth.

Which made him shake with the effort not to follow suit. He cleared his throat. "Yes, well, attack birds."

"Pardon me?" Miss Tanning looked immediately skeptical. As she should. He'd chosen an intelligent woman to woo and not just a wealthy one.

At that moment, a strong scent of rose wafted over to him, and he and Lady Felicity exchanged looks and slowly turned to look behind them.

Miss Tittering approached. "Oh my dear, yes. Attack birds. Pooped in his eye, dripping down his face when I saw him."

All eight people at the tables gasped and looked from Abraham to Lady Felicity and back. Then Abraham scoffed. "Miss Tittering, surely such a tale is far-fetched?"

"Not at all. You were there as my witness, you and Miss Bumbly."

"Who?"

Lady Felicity stood up. "Oh, Miss Tittering, it's so fortuitous you have arrived. Would you take my spot?"

Abraham jerked to his feet. He waved across the room. "Lord Bellingham. Would you mind?"

Abraham offered his arm to Lady Felicity as they made their way as sedately as possible back to the needlepoint. It was blessedly empty at the moment.

He meant to leave her to her stitching, but when her body shook and the frailness of her hands and arms hung helplessly at her side, he sat in the closest chair. "Do show me your stitching."

CHAPTER 8

*F*elicity tried to breathe normally. What did Lord Ridgecrest mean, bringing up their childhood and hinting at the lowness of her mother's station. Why lash out as he had? Did he think she'd given away his secrets to Lord Bolton?

Another thing settled uncomfortably in her gut: his marked attention to Miss Tanning. Did he feel that he, too, was too elevated for the likes of Felicity? She squeezed her eyes tight, hoping to grasp hold of her last chance at a respectable marriage but watching it slip away.

"Oh, now, Lady Felicity. Please don't." Lord Bolton handed her his handkerchief.

She took it. "I'm just being silly."

"Not at all. I'd do the same, only my tears would not fall in such a lovely manner."

Her eyes lifted to his and the enhanced color struck him again.

"I think Ridgecrest is daft to behave as he is. And you are rightly affected."

She nodded, dabbing her eyes.

"You're lovely, you know." His face was lined with concern, sincerity filling his voice with intensity.

She almost started crying again, only this time in response to his tender regard.

He lifted his hand as though to touch her face but he lowered it before it could. "Now, would you show me a few more of your stitches? Please?"

"I thought you said this was only for the mothers and grand-mothers."

"If you'll recall, I also mentioned how much I enjoyed your stitches."

She eyed him with no small amount of skepticism. But she began again, pulling the needle up and through her stitches.

He watched over her back, attentive, the gentle puffs of his breath every now and then tickling her neck. "Would you teach me?"

"What!" She looked around. Everyone else in the room seemed distracted with their own activities. "You can't really want to learn."

"I most certainly do." He moved closer. "The first thing I must know: how you know where to poke the needle so that it comes up precisely where you want it to?"

She shook her head. "Oh, but it doesn't. See. You must play with it a little, like so." She poked the needle through to the front a few times to show it moving closer.

"Ah, but you don't usually have so many attempts, surely."

"Well, no." She tilted her head. "Once you've done it for as many hours, as most of us have, you become more accurate on your first guess."

"That's quite impressive to me. Please. I'd love to watch you for a time. Show me how you manage it."

Charmed, she made several stitches in the greenery of the flowers, showing him smaller and larger designs. She couldn't imagine he cared, but he seemed as interested as she'd ever seen him. And she was so grateful for the distraction.

"See that bit there. When you add the darker color, it makes the leaves stand out."

She smiled. "It's an art, really. Few appreciate the work involved, but all enjoy the end result."

"May I try?" His boyish expression made her smile.

"If you'd like."

"You don't think I'll mess it up, do you?"

"I won't let you. We do plan to leave this with the Garveys, you know."

"I should like to think I will have contributed."

She did not believe a word of it, but she was grateful for his efforts to entertain her.

He held the tiny needle in his large hands and nearly dropped it twice before he brought it back behind the stitches and poked it forward.

"Oh, not quite." She reached underneath to help guide his hand. As her fingers wrapped around his, she had an absurd desire to take off her gloves. Their closeness felt intimate; an overwhelming urge to rest her cheek on his shoulder filled her. How nice it would be to sit thus, with him, for many an afternoon in the quiet of their own home. She gulped down the shocking direction of her thoughts. And yet, she could never imagine Lord Ridgecrest and she doing anything similar.

While she continued to guide Lord Bolton's hand, his voice murmured softly. "Tell me."

"What?"

"Tell me why Ridgecrest behaved as he did."

She sighed and considered how to respond. "I imagine he might be embarrassed by some of the memories associated with our family."

"With good reason?"

She tipped her head. "Perhaps."

"But why lash out?"

"One time, when he was a lad, my mother saved him from an awful moment with his father. I was playing the piano forte. I remember it so clearly still for I'd never seen such violence acted upon another person." She shook her head and refused to look away from their needlepoint. "My mother went out there, full of thunder and soon he was in the parlor with a plate of biscuits, listening to me play."

He was quiet for so long she turned to search his face. His kind eyes warmed her toes.

She had not seen young Lord Ridgecrest again after that day. She'd heard he'd gone straight to school and was rarely home for holiday. She'd been glad for him and secretly a little disappointed for herself.

Lord Bolton paused and then poked a needle up through the fabric. He was getting better. Felicity smiled.

He seemed to consider carefully his next words. "And have you reason to be embarrassed?"

She shook her head. "Not by a particular memory, no."

"But general association?"

"I suppose you could say that." Did she dare share her plight with him? What if the lower station of her mother's family were to get out amongst the party attendees? She knew it wouldn't be a secret long kept, but if she could but find marriage before it was widely known, she would be forgiven. Perhaps.

"I cannot abide the man for what he said to you. But if you must persist in hoping for his hand, I will tell you a happy secret."

"What? What is it?"

"He has looked over here no less than five times since we began talking."

"What?"

"It's true. Perhaps he is wondering why you and I are so close?"

She almost jerked away, but he said. "No, stay close. I do believe we might succeed in making the pair of them jealous."

"Can I look?"

"Better not."

Perhaps he was correct. If an obvious show of her choice was not being perceived in the most accurate manner, perhaps she would win Lord Ridgecrest by design. She shook her head. Never did she ever see herself as those conniving women described in Fordyce's sermons, and yet here she was. "I believe you are a bad influence on me, Lord Bolton."

"You're smiling while you say such awful things."

"Because I do believe I like it."

His grin was all the reward she needed.

Her slow rise of one brow fascinated him. "It's not entirely *im*proper, you see."

"Decidedly not. We are well within the grey area between proper and improper."

She laughed. Then pointed to the needlework. "And your stitches. You're a natural." She narrowed her eyes. "Are you certain you've never done this before?"

"Quite." He coughed.

She was enjoying his attention much more than she thought she ever would. "Are you finished?"

He handed her the needle. "I am. Tell me what you think. Will you have to pick out what I've done?" His insecurity was endearing. She leaned closer so she could see, even though she'd already had a perfectly clear view. His smell of spices filled the air around them.

She shifted, aware of every movement, feeling sensations in the air between them. She pretended to study his stitches, the feel of his breath on her face and she leaned closer. Her arm brushed his as she pointed. "Oh dear."

"Oh no, what did I do?"

She smiled and turned to him, her face closer than she realized it would be. "I tease you. They're wonderful. My mother and my governess would be proud." She studied him, his handsome face, the twinkle in his eyes, and was suddenly very glad she had met him.

"You know me, the love of every governess and grandmother."

She imagined a great deal many more women loved or would love him, and they were most assuredly *not* the governesses. She remembered Miss Hastings talking about him being penniless and thought that a great shame. "I imagine a great deal many more women would love you." She sucked in her breath and turned away, her face flaming.

But he just laughed. "Oh, the things you say. I don't have much to recommend me."

She wondered about that. "What are we going to do about Miss Tittering? She just told everyone she thinks I'm Miss Bumbly."

He laughed. "I quite enjoy the confusion, I must admit."

"Did you see the faces of the others? I confess I wasn't looking."

"I confess I was more concerned about other matters." He poked his finger. "Ow." He stuck a finger in his mouth. "But I will clear that up right now." He stood.

"Wait, what are you going to do?"

"I don't know." He waited for her to stand and join him, then they walked back toward their group, who were in the middle of a new game of whist, Lord Ridgecrest not looking pleased. "I believe our Lord Ridgecrest does not enjoy his present company?"

He looked like he enjoyed Miss Tanning's company plenty. "Or perhaps he doesn't enjoy losing?"

He held a finger to his nose. "I believe you've hit upon it."

They watched for a moment, and then Lord Bolton moved to stand behind Miss Tittering. "I believe I was mistaken about something earlier on the beach."

They continued in hushed conversation that Felicity longed to hear until Lord Ridgecrest addressed her. He stood and joined her at her side. "I wonder if you would like to walk with me tomorrow?"

"Yes, I'd like that very much."

"After your piano forte playing, perhaps?"

She looked down, remembering his strange behavior. "I'm unsure why Lord Bolton brought up the piano forte. I did not tell him. About . . . anything."

"I know. Just the mention of you on a piano brought such a rush of memories that I felt unsettled. Forgive me."

"Of course." Perhaps she would still have a chance at winning his heart? She lifted her lashes to see into his face and for a moment saw a flash of something—interest? Her attention was drawn to Lord Bolton's conversation with Miss Tittering. And everything suddenly felt less clear than it had ever been.

Later that night, she couldn't sleep. The house was unaccountably cold. They had had little wood and a short stub of a candle. Remembering Mrs. Daw and her promise of food in the kitchen, she went in search of the woman, her candle flickering precariously with what might be her last flame.

Conversation in the kitchen sounded warm, friendly. Mrs. Daw's cheerful laugh lit a friendly path through Felicity, and she hurried down the hall toward the sound. When she entered, the flickering light from the fireplace lit the corner of the room where Mrs. Daw and the married woman she'd seen earlier sat together.

"Come in, Lady Felicity. I hoped you'd come."

"Oh, thank you, Mrs. Daw."

"This is Lady Anslowe, wife of Lord Anslowe. Both are guests at the party."

Lady Anslowe's soft smile matched the room, and Felicity liked her immediately. "Please, my friends call me Emmeline."

"Oh, I could never." Felicity rested a hand at her heart. "Oh, I mean, of course we must be friends, but I think I would feel more comfortable using titles."

"If you must. But really, Emmeline would be lovely. I quite like my first name."

Felicity considered her. "I prefer my second. No one knows it. Honora. My first name's Felicity, which of course no one else uses either. Everyone calls me Lady Felicity."

Lady Anslowe, her dark hair coming loose from its pins, was holding the most glorious thing Felicity had seen since she arrived at Havencrest.

"I'm so pleased to meet you, um Emmeline. May I ask, how did you get such a beautiful candle?"

She laughed. "Oh, Mrs. Garvey is my husband's aunt, and he knew what to expect. He packed accordingly."

What an odd thing to do.

"We have far more than we need. I'll see that we share."

"Oh, you are a friend indeed."

Mrs. Daw patted the chair beside her. "Come in, come in." She moved the plate of biscuits closer to Felicity. "Have some tea, and I've made extra biscuits."

Felicity joined them, and already her confusion felt less.

Mrs. Daw handed her a cup of tea. "You've having quite a quandary, aren't you?"

She replaced her cup. "I am?"

"Well certainly. Do you choose your heart or your head?"

Felicity's feelings of happy expectation fizzled somewhat. "I'm sure I don't understand."

Mrs. Daw patted her hand. "Of course you don't, but don't you worry. Everything will work out."

Felicity bit a biscuit, savoring the nourishment. Their dinner had been sparse. She looked pointedly at the woman sitting across from her and back at Mrs. Daw.

Mrs. Daw followed her gaze. "You are in excellent company. Lady Anslowe here, she's in a quandary herself."

"Pardon me?" Emmeline widened her eyes. "Am I?"

Mrs. Daw continued as if the woman hadn't spoken. "But her husband is handsome. I remember talk of him when he was single. Just about every young lady had her eye on that one." She clucked. "You're a lucky one, but then he is too, I'd say."

Emmeline sipped her tea, a noncommittal mumble at her lips. Then she said, "Thank you."

Then Emmeline rested her teacup. "I'm happy to meet you, Lady Honora." She winked, and Felicity thought her the most wonderful person at the party. "I saw you at your needlepoint and wished we'd already formed an acquaintance." Her eyes shone with sincerity, and Felicity liked her more.

"I as well. You might want to add your stitches to that needlepoint while you are here. It is to be given as a gift to the Garveys before we leave."

"At house party end? Do you suppose we'll finish it?"

"I for one hope so. I do not like to leave things unfinished."

"Yes, it is bothersome. And now I'm torn between beginning such a thing at all and then feeling that irksome sensation as I drive away knowing that it shall never be completed or aiding in the effort."

"I recommend aiding in the effort since I myself am already trapped into its completion."

Emmeline laughed.

Mrs. Daw sat back in her chair, resting her hands folded across her front. "Where is Mrs. Dotting?"

"She's been enjoying herself with the other ladies, I do believe. But at the present, she is asleep."

"Feel free to bring back a biscuit for her if you'd like."

"I'm sure she'd appreciate it."

They ate in companionable silence, and Felicity sipped her tea. Then Mrs. Daw patted her hand. "We must get you sorted with the right man."

Felicity froze and replaced her teacup with a trembling hand. "I don't find this conversation necessary." She squeezed Mrs. Daw's hand that still rested on her arm. "I do appreciate the sentiment, but I'm so highly uncomfortable discussing such things."

"Oh, never you mind. Lady Anslowe is superb at keeping secrets. Aren't you dear?"

Before Lady Anslowe could respond, Mrs. Daw continued, "I'll give it some thought and keep my eyes open, and you come back to talk to me." She seemed so sure of herself. Mrs. Dotting never quite knew what would be best, and her mother was no longer with them. Felicity suddenly yearned for the kind of chats she could have with this woman. And then without warning, tears sprung to her eyes and there was nothing she could do to hide the few that overflowed down her cheeks. "Oh, I do apologize."

Emmeline reached across and handed her a handkerchief.

Mrs. Daw immediately rose to put her arm around Felicity's shoulder, and then it all came out in a wave. "I just don't know what to do. I don't know how to manage. My mother isn't here." She dabbed her eyes, knowing that even if her mother were here, she just wouldn't know how to manage in the ton. She never had. She complained often enough of their high-nosed practices. Often her mother's advice was full of things Felicity wished she could do but knew if she ever did, she might be ostracized forever. Didn't her mother know that reputation mattered for most people? Her mother had been lucky to marry a man of title.

"I just need to secure him." She wished she could bite her tongue off and take back her last words. It sounded so mercenary when spoken aloud to strangers.

Mrs. Daw shook her head. "Come now. Don't you wish to marry for love?"

"I understand." Emmeline's eyes were full of sympathy.

"You do?"

"Certainly. Sometimes our only recourse is to marry well."

Mrs. Daw shook her head. "But you're a titled lady. Surely you have some choice in the matter."

Felicity nodded. "I do. But because of my family situation, I need to marry someone respectable. A solid family name is the most important."

Mrs. Daw refilled her teacup. "You're in the right place, dearie. All the men at this party are perfectly respectable. Remember, no one is beyond reproach, my dear. But the men here are all well regarded. The Garveys have their limits."

Emmeline and Felicity shared a look.

"Uncle Garvey is a dear man," Emmeline said. "And Aunt Garvey runs such a beautiful home here. It's been so long since I've been to any activity outside my local neighbors, I appreciate the invitation."

"But surely some are truly above reproach while others might be not quite proper but not improper either . . ." She waited, holding her breath for some reason. Why did it matter if they agreed with Lord Bolton?

Mrs. Daw smiled. "Exactly. You've figured it out."

Felicity leaned forward. "Perhaps I can beg a confidence of you both, ask for your advice on a matter?" Emmeline had such a solid presence of mind about her, and Mrs. Daw charmed her way into Felicity's trust. "There is a man here who I have most desperately hoped would begin to notice, to perhaps form an alliance."

"A Lord Bolton, if I'm not mistaken."

Felicity sucked in her breath. *Not Lord Bolton.* There was a mischievous twinkle in Mrs. Daw's eyes. Felicity began to shake her head.

"Oh, he is a dear. He's quite the most respectable in his family, charming. And in desperate need of a wife."

Felicity cleared her throat. "Desperate need?"

"Oh yes, his brother has gambled away the family wealth, and he's now bound to find a handsome dowry to refill the coffers and save the estate."

Felicity covered her mouth with one hand.

"Oh, come now, let's not pretend we don't understand how it works. You best wise up, and quickly, if you're gonna play the game with no one but Mrs. Dotting to advise you."

"I was hoping for more along the lines of—"

Mrs. Daw waved her hand. "Lord Bolton will be a wonderful match."

"You are mistaken, I'm sure. I have my eyes on someone completely different. He is quite the perfect gentleman. For me." Even as she said the words, she wondered if they were true. Why had Mrs. Daw thought Felicity was so fully enamored with Lord Bolton? Of all people. Their close conversations, his marked attention, would be perceived in absolutely the wrong manner. She stood. "I must go."

"Oh, if you wish, dear." Mrs. Daw's secretive smile bothered Felicity more than it should. Perhaps having a woman confidante was overrated.

Mrs. Daw stood. "I'm not really sure why your heart and head don't simply choose the same man."

Felicity curtseyed to them both as she left. "Thank you again Mrs. Daw."

"Come back and visit any time."

"Good night, Lady Honora," Emmeline said.

Of all the terrible quandaries to be in. She left the kitchen before she could respond. She needed to go to Lord Bolton straight away. Drastic measures were needed.

CHAPTER 9

*L*ord Bolton couldn't sleep. His mind plagued him with thoughts of Lady Felicity. The woman who was actively pursuing another man, the woman who might not have a penny to her name, a woman who beguiled him like no other. "She could be my ruin."

He paced in his room. "Focus, man. You must." He cursed his brother again. It was nothing new, but the words came out with more venom than usual. Could he even win Lady Felicity if he were free to do so? If she were miraculously wealthy and available to him? Could he win her heart? He thought about her fixated purpose in attracting Ridgecrest, and he wasn't sure he could dissuade her from her purpose—not because she was impervious to Abraham, but because she was singularly stubborn.

But he knew nothing else about her. He'd heard nothing of her family. She hadn't been present for most of the season by her own admission.

The walls of his room closed tighter around him. He had much too energy. Craving the outdoors or a brisk walk through the halls, perhaps the conservatory even in the dark of night. He placed his hand to open the door. Voices in the hall outside his door stopped him.

"Lord Ridgecrest. I. What are you doing up so late?"

"The same as you, perhaps. Couldn't sleep? Looking for some company?"

Her small gasp made Abraham smile.

"Come now, no need to be missish with me. We are too intimate for such modesty."

"I don't understand." The catch in Lady Felicity's voice drove Abraham to action. He flung open his door.

Both jumped in front of him.

He leaned against his doorframe, arms crossed his chest. "What do we have here?"

"Nothing!" Felicity's face really was quite charming when she blushed.

Ridgecrest dipped his head. "Excuse me."

Felicity watched him until he turned the corner. "Oh, thank heavens. We must converse." She looked up and down the hallway and then tugged at his arm to follow her.

"I'm not sure what to think, my lady."

"You can stop thinking whatever gives you that tone."

"What tone?"

"The one where you sound so inviting. You know that's not what this is."

"I'm even more intrigued. What are you alluding to? I must know. That's not what this is?" He rubbed his chin. "Do I sound inviting?" He couldn't help but enjoy a few moments pestering her.

She pulled him into an alcove. "You're always teasing, always tempting."

"Tempting?"

"But what do you offer, really?"

"What do I—"

"Precisely. You are all in fun. You're good at . . ." She waved her arms around, whipping him in the nose.

"Watch the eye."

Laughing, she pressed a hand to his chest. "You're accomplished at making a woman feel a certain way…But you. Don't mean a single word of it." She stepped nearer, her face close enough to kiss. "Do you?"

He swallowed, his heart pounding under her palm.

She pressed more firmly into the area above his heart, her face changing. Questions filled her expression. "Do you?"

He stared back at her and for a moment, nothing mattered at all but this moment, he stepped nearer, covered her hand with his own over his chest. He reached a hand up and ran his thumb along her jawline. She closed her eyes, her face leaning into his palm.

"You see?" She murmured, her lips curled in pure enjoyment.

Abraham couldn't have moved if he'd wanted to, so entranced was he by Lady Felicity's upturned face. He ran his thumb back toward her ear and down her neckline. Her mouth turned up into a small smile, curling in a delicious dip on her upper lip. And at once all he wanted was to place his mouth right over that dip, tasting her softness.

But he swallowed twice and tried to clear his mind. His lips had never touched another's. He guessed hers hadn't either. Could he be the first to kiss her, when neither of them knew a clear path ahead? "You asked me a question I find impossible to answer. Do I mean what I say? Unfortunately, I'm not at liberty to make decisions based on matters of the heart."

Her eyes fluttered open. She blinked twice, and then clarity returned. And she nodded. "I am under the same restrictions." Her forehead wrinkled in an adorable frown. "Perhaps." She looked away. "I don't know. I wish I had someone to advise me." Then she sucked in her breath and stepped farther away, straightened her skirts, and then lifted her chin. She reminded him so much of the stiff and proper lady he'd met on the beach, he almost laughed.

"I have requested an audience with you because people are talking." She looked away. "About us. The housekeeper."

"Mrs. Daw?"

"Yes, she's of the impression we've formed an understanding. Others have asked me, that horrible Miss Hastings being one."

"I don't think I've ever heard you be less than generous."

"You're correct. She might not be horrible to some."

"What do they say? About us?"

"That we're to be a match. That we are compatible." She blushed furiously. "That we are a love." Her face flamed, and she looked away.

His smile grew, then faltered. He was equally enchanted and disturbed. On the one hand, he found Lady Felicity more and more enticing, and on the other, he knew he should be spending time trying to win Miss Tanning. She was his surest manner in which to save his estate and marry to improve his situation.

His hand still covered hers. Though she'd stepped away, she hadn't removed it. He cradled her hand in his, caressing her bare fingers before he brought them to his lips.

Touching her skin with his mouth tingled his lips with a wonderous sensation. He found great difficulty in limiting the kiss to just one. "This talk is hurting your plans for Lord Perfect."

She snorted. "And yours for Miss Wealthy."

"That's not the only reason I am seeking her hand."

"It's not?"

"No, she has an ancient noble line, excellent heritage. She might help erase the damage my brother's done to our family name."

Her face twisted in discomfort.

"And Lord Perfect. Is he everything you want?"

"Of. . .course."

"So what do you propose we do? Stage a parting of ways?"

"I don't know. I was hoping you could help me with two urgent matters. Firstly, no one must know that you and I are . . . they can't misunderstand that you and I . . ." She looked away.

"What are we?"

"I don't know. It doesn't matter, does it?"

"Hmmm. And your other matter . . . ?"

"What can I do? I need further assistance in convincing him. Lord Ridgecrest at times . . . he seems like he might be interested."

Abraham felt an odd desire to growl. "He would have escorted you somewhere quiet tonight if I hadn't stepped outside my door." His voice came out more irritated than he'd meant but much less irritated than he felt. She deserved someone much better than Ridgecrest. "What do you need from this man?"

"His respectability. Same as you said. His is an ancient family line, his impeccable reputation would help my family's faltering one."

Abraham's heart sank, knowing his own family reputation could do nothing to elevate anyone's. "He didn't sound respectable to me. You'd have been caught in a scandal." He stood taller. "What would you have done? Followed him? Drug *him* to some dark corner?"

She shook her head. "Of course not."

He held his hands out. "Yet here we are." His irritation rose. He tried to tamp it, but it wouldn't be bridled.

She turned away.

"Perhaps you need to take a look at what is respectable and what is not. Or *perhaps* lower your respectability standards a little bit, or see what is right in front of you." Where was his anger coming from? He was suddenly so irrationally angry that she could not see what a disreputable rake Ridgecrest really was and . . . his thoughts shuddered to a stop. *And* she couldn't see what a good man he was. When the thought rested on him, he saw in such an obvious manner his own feelings. "Or perhaps you're more concerned about perceived respectability than looking for a truly respectable person?" His breathing came faster, and his face stiffened. He stared her down, willing her to respond, to explain, to see what he was trying to explain.

But instead, her lip quivered, her face fell, and she ran from him, down the hall, around the corner and out of sight. And she took with her the only candle, small though it was. The hallway filled with darkness, as bleak as his hope.

CHAPTER 10

$\mathcal{T}$he wind hammered against her window. The fire embers burned coldly in the grate. Morning would begin in moments, but Felicity could find little motivation to leave her room. Perhaps if she could wear a blanket over her head? How utterly ridiculous her thoughts, but her urge to hide burned stronger than her need for a disappointing breakfast. And so she was sorely tempted to skip the meal altogether, to skip the activities, to never leave this room.

Why must she hide? Lord Bolton. Lord Ridgecrest—no, she sought Lord Ridgecrest, and she hid from Lord Bolton. His warm eyes came to mind. Why was she hiding from Lord Bolton? Because people thought they were together.

She paced her room. No, that wasn't precisely correct. She hid from Lord Bolton because she fancied him. No, she corrected again, she was unaccountably and unreasonably in love with the man. She gasped out a sob. No. Perhaps not love. But she did prefer his company to all others. Her heart hammered inside as she realized the truth of her words. She wrapped her arms around her middle, squeezing her eyes against anything so irrational as another tear. Could she have developed feelings for Lord Bolton in so short a time?

But she hid from Lord Ridgecrest as well, didn't she? What had he been doing in the hallway in the dark hours of night? She snorted to herself. He might wonder the same of her. For a moment, she'd been hopeful. His eyes had filled with interest, a different kind, something in the brown depths sharpened, and their glint surprised her. And then the tiniest feather of fear had nudged her. Lord Bolton, stepping out into the hallway when he did, had felt like the rays of sun after a brisk and chilly walk.

She walked to the window, watching the sun's rays begin to swell on the horizon. Was Lord Ridgecrest a good and honorable man? Were respectability and honor two different things entirely?

Never had she considered such a thing, that the eyes of the ton would revere someone without honor, that someone might have an impeccable reputation and not be entirely trustworthy.

But Lord Ridgecrest, surely he would never have misused a moment in a dark hallway. Lord Bolton seemed to think he might have.

And hadn't she? Dragged Lord Bolton to a small alcove herself? Stood close enough to embrace, even kiss the man? She leaned her flushed skin against the cool glass of her window. What a heathen she was. Perhaps she was the lower-class hoyden they suspected her mother of being. When his heart pounded beneath her hand, she felt her own match its pace, and suddenly nothing else seemed to matter, not in the whole world, expect for Lord Bolton, face turned down to hers in the low light of a flickering candle. Hoyden or not, she might never forget that moment, ever.

Her parents had been truly happy. She thought of them, their stolen moments together when they thought she was unaware. Her mother's eyes, adoring her father in every way, and he in his tender regard, loving her right back. They had laughed together. So often Felicity had thought them too brazen, too demonstrative. Her own governess had taught her not to behave so. But . . . she considered their faces, the joy in their lives. She yearned for the same.

The ordered expectation and pieces of her life were not falling together quite as they ought.

She dressed without her maid, putting on her warmest clothing—a pelisse, an extra wrap, a scarf, and a muff—and made her way downstairs. The wind whistled through the eaves, and she looked forward to the brisk awakening she might receive out of doors.

She needed it, an awakening. She had to think. Her mother held many members of the ton in disdain. Felicity had always assumed that they did not associate with other peers because her mother did not desire their company. Then her governess led her to believe it was because her mother would not be welcome. But the more Felicity considered her earlier years, the more she suspected she had been initially correct that the distance was motivated by her mother's choice in company. She'd heard her say, so often, "I wish to associate with people of true valor. Where can we find them? They are all around us here in Haversham."

And so they had stayed sequestered, enjoying their neighbors, their tenants, her mother's and father's true friends.

All the while, Felicity grew restless to make her way in the world, to find a respectable man of the ton to marry, to erase the tarnish of her mother's family, of their money from trade. Of her nontraditional ways.

Felicity pushed open the door to the outside, and the wind slammed the door back into her. She stepped out into the wind and struggled to pull the door shut once more. A servant approached, a footman, who helped her close it.

Then she turned, welcoming the wild tempestuous weather. What if her governess was more wrong and her mother more correct? What was so wrong about a woman marrying above her station?

She shook her head. Too much to understand in this one moment. She pushed against the wind. The waves crashed furiously, white tips blowing away in the air around them, mist rising up everywhere below. She suspected she'd be drenched the moment she set foot near the water. She turned and walked farther away from the estate, away from the water, toward a grove of trees on the opposite side of the property. She'd heard of a stream, a path, perhaps some shelter from the wind.

The sun had risen but was in such a haze, little warmth made its way through her outer layers. Wind whipped stronger, and the trees ahead of her bent. She felt the first raindrop.

"Oh no." She turned. Dark clouds filled the sky behind her, moving in. The clouds opened up, and water fell down in sheets. She ran for cover under the trees, slipping on the grass on her way, stumbling up again and scrambling for cover.

She hugged the area closest to a tree trunk and felt fewer drops from above but was hit by a considerable amount coming at her side from the wind. She wrapped her arms around her middle and crouched down at the base of the tree, ducking her head in her elbows. The shivers started within a few moments.

Loud claps of thunder shattered the air around her. She pulled her knees up as close to her body as they would go.

Shouts sounded from the house, carrying as though distant, on the wind. She stood, peering through the trees. A man on horseback came barreling across the open grass.

She ran out from her cover, waving her arms, and he waved back. She squinted. Who had come?

When he came through the rain and she could recognize him, she gasped. "Lord Ridgecrest."

He brought his horse to a stop, ran to her. "Are you all right? They alerted us to your location just as the rain began to fall. I apologize it's taken me so long."

Her teeth chattered. "Th-Thank you."

He led her to his horse, placed his hands around her waist, and lifted her up. Then he jumped up behind her, wrapping his arms around her to take the reins. "You're freezing. Let's get you back and warm."

She nodded, hoping to feel the warmth of their bodies, hoping to start to warm, but her skin was cold, her insides were cold, and nothing could penetrate. She dipped her head against the rain pelting at her face and pressed her lips together to stop her teeth from chattering and vibrating inside her head.

They rushed to the house and were there in moments. She slid off the horse into the arms of Mrs. Daw. "Good heavens, child. Come inside."

Mrs. Garvey stood in the doorway, ushering them in. "Please add extra wood to the kitchen fire. We must warm her." Her face looked pinched, concerned. Felicity paused the hurried steps of Mrs. Daw so Felicity could turn toward their hostess. "Thank you, Mrs. Garvey."

"You're welcome."

They ushered her into the kitchen, sat her right in front of the fire. Soon it was blazing. The added blankets they wrapped around her shoulders and the fire helped the shivering to subside. Mrs. Daw carried over a warmed cup of broth. "There now, my lady. Sip this. It'll warm you in no time."

Felicity tried to grasp the cup, soak up its warmth in her fingers, but her hands shook still, and she didn't trust herself.

"Allow me?" Lord Ridgecrest had joined her. He sat at her side and lifted the cup in his hands. His eyes were caring, concerned. He sat close, lifting the cup to her mouth. "May I?"

She nodded, not taking her eyes off his face. The warmth of the cup at her lips felt comforting; the man, watching her mouth so intently, was intoxicating. But she felt strangely distant. The broth was delicious, and she welcomed its warmth.

Mrs. Dotting arrived, flushed. "Oh, my lady! Good heavens!"

Felicity's insides twisted in guilt. She should have let Mrs. Dotting know where she would be, should have waited until a decent hour, probably should never have gone outside in the first place.

Mrs. Dotting took in the scene and then wisely hushed while she sat near. "Oh, my poppet. What will I tell your father?"

Lord Ridgecrest lifted the cup again to Felicity's lips, and she finished the contents of the cup. "Thank you," she whispered. "For all of it."

He tucked a wet strand of her hair behind her ear. "I was grateful for the opportunity. The hope that I could spare you motivated me."

Her heart warmed at the thought. And at last she felt some of the cold dissipate. "I don't know what I would have done if you hadn't come."

"Your mother did much the same for me, in a manner of speaking." He rested a hand on top of her head. "I'll come see how you are later?"

She nodded. "I'd like that."

He stood.

Mrs. Dotting immediately took his place. "Let's get you up and in your bed."

Felicity admitted that sounded like just the thing. As she made her way upstairs, allowed her maid to dress her again for bed, and even as she pulled her coverlet high up to her chin, her mind was alive with thoughts of Lord Ridgecrest. Could she have done it? Won him over?

She closed her eyes, sleep calling to her more easily than she would have thought. But her last thoughts were not of Lord Ridgecrest, but rather of the strong heartbeat of Lord Bolton, pounding against her hand. She wondered what it would have been like if he had cradled her up on a horse, riding through the rain.

CHAPTER 11

*A*braham entered breakfast, and the room went strangely quiet. Miss Hastings snickered to Lady Anslowe, who refused to respond. Miss Tanning watched him closer than ever. He went to the sideboard and filled his plate with some measly offerings. He felt eyes on him, and no one in the room had yet spoken since he arrived. He turned to take his seat, "Good morning." He nodded to the room at large.

Miss Tinsdale leaned closer as he lifted the first bite to his mouth. "I'm terribly sorry. Moments like these map our disappointments."

He swallowed slowly. "Excuse me?"

"Lady Felicity."

"What has happened?" His alarm grew. "Is she well?"

"Oh yes, I believe so. She's had quite a time of it, cold right through. I hear she'll be abed today and they're hoping she won't be taken by fever."

He looked around the room. They appeared mostly sympathetic at his expense.

Miss Hastings leaned forward conspiratorially. "Lord Ridgecrest rode down the property in the rain, placed her on his horse, and rode back. I hear they were together in the kitchen and that he has visited her room asking after her twice already."

Abraham's mind was aflood with emotion. And he was well aware of the intent manner in which everyone was watching for his reaction. "I am so sorry to hear it. I hope she will be well." He sipped his tea. "We can all be grateful for Lord Ridgecrest. I can think of no man she'd rather have at her side in a moment of distress."

Miss Tinsdale's eyes filled with sympathy, and he could not abide another moment of false caring. Then others, including Lord Bellingham, entered the room, and soon the conversation turned to much more neutral topics. But Abraham's mind was racing with thoughts. Lady Felicity ill. They were worried about fevers. And Lord Ridgecrest. He almost growled in the back of his throat as he imaged that man's arms around Lady Felicity on the back of a horse. He could not abide the thought, and suddenly, he cared less for his estate and more for himself. The mistress of his estate could also be the mistress of his heart, even if she didn't bring with her a penny.

It was time he made his intentions clear. He stood. What were his intentions, exactly? He didn't know. He sat back down. Mr. Cavanaugh, who sat opposite, eyed him, then asked another question of Sir Richard, something about crops in India. Abraham stared at his food and then couldn't stomach it. He stood again.

Everyone noticed, but he paid them no mind, nodded to the room at large, and then walked with purpose out the door. Once he'd cleared their training eyes, he picked up his pace and took the stairs two at a time. He stopped a passing maid. "Would you tell me where to find Lady Felicity? I hear she is unwell."

"Aye, my lord. And she's being doted on, make no mistake." She pointed and explained which room was Lady Felicity's and then curtseyed to his back as he hurried away.

He rounded a corner and then slowed immediately. Ridgecrest. Watching Lord Ridgecrest exit Lady Felicity's room set his blood burning. When he passed, the man's smirk made Abraham ill. But neither said anything, Abraham's nod in greeting was the briefest he could muster.

His feet moved slower in the dim hallway, her door barring him from doing anything to alleviate her suffering. Her door that welcomed Ridgecrest. He stood outside, not knowing his purpose. Dash. He should have brought something, anything. Flowers. A biscuit from breakfast? No, that would have cheered no one. A book. He nodded to himself. He would go find her a book to read.

The sounds of movement inside stalled his exit. Really, he just wanted to see her. How was she? Was a fever imminent, like the intrusive Miss Hastings suggested? The door opened, and he moved to get a good view of her bed. He sucked in a breath. Lady Felicity. Her cheeks were rosy, her face flushed, but she appeared to be well enough. His shoulders relaxed in a great sense of relief. Just as the door was closing, her eyes raised to meet his gaze. Then the door shut. Mrs. Garvey cleared her throat.

"Oh, I beg your leave." He bowed. "Is she well?"

Mrs. Garvey waved her hand. "Perfectly well. Eating the foods I suggest and some of my elderberry wine will restore her much quicker than calling the doctor, who will only swallow up our money, nod a few times, and take his leave."

Abraham nodded. "Thank you, for your care." As she turned to leave, he stammered. "Might I?" He indicated the door.

"Enter her room?" Mrs. Garvey's eyebrows rose up to her hairline, and she somehow managed to look down her nose at his tall person. "I should think not. Not while I cannot attend you."

He dipped his head. "Just so. Thank you."

Her face softened. "But if you wish to send in a message or other gift, I'm certain one of the maids would be happy to deliver it."

"Yes. Thank you." His heart picked up. A mission to the library to fetch Lady Felicity a book would be just the thing.

He walked through the hallways toward the library with a singular purpose. Somehow Miss Tanning mattered less and less. But what if he followed his heart and Lady Felicity would not choose him? That was a risk he would have to take. He had to try. Dash it all. Dash his chances with Miss Tanning, dash his whole estate, he had to try. He gulped. And hoped that she would accept his suit and hoped she would have something for them to live on in her dowry.

The library was empty, so he made his way down the aisles of books. What would she enjoy? He cursed the fact that he didn't know. He wished to know everything about her, her whims, her every wish. But at the moment, he would try to find something entertaining. The books were mostly old, scholarly. He was impressed with the library. Mr. Garvey cleared his throat behind Abraham.

"Oh, just the man I was hoping to see."

"Could I help you find a title?"

"Yes, for a young lady. She's been caught in this infernal wind and a short downfall of rain."

"I have just the thing. Have you heard of Jane Austen? *Sense and Sensibility* was her first."

Abraham had not, but he grinned. "If you suggest it to be of value to the ladies, I will gladly borrow it in her behalf."

"It is her newest I think she will most enjoy. *Pride and Prejudice.*" He moved along a row of books. "Here." He reached up, dusted off the top of a small volume, and handed it to Abraham.

"Thank you. I'm in your debt. I admit to being at quite a loss." He glanced up at the books. "I see you are a scholar of war strategy."

"Yes, I've also been following Wellington."

"That's a drawing room discussion I'd love to have. Perhaps later this evening."

"I'll be here. Join me." Mr. Garvey nodded to him and left Abraham to his own plans.

He sat at a desk across the room, searched out an inkwell and pen, but was at a loss to find paper. He sat back. What house did not keep sheets of paper in their library desks? He searched further, then eyed the wall of books. Surely, somewhere would be a few sheaves. It was a library, after all. A small voice made him jump. He whirled around to see who else had happened upon him unawares. "Lady Anslowe?"

"Yes." She smiled. "Sorry to startle you."

"I had no idea a library could hide so many individuals. I thought I was alone." He bowed. "I apologize for my jump."

"I couldn't help but notice you are searching for something." She indicated his inkwell. "Perhaps a sheaf of paper or parchment?" She held up her stack. "I would be happy to share."

"Oh, thank you. You've come right at the most opportune moment."

She handed him two. "Are you working on something special?" She walked closer to his desk. "*Pride and Prejudice*. One of my favorites. Are you reading it?"

He chuckled. What could he say to this? "I would enjoy reading it, but it is a gift. I thought a young lady confined to her room might like something to read."

"Ah, for Lady Felicity."

"Are you much acquainted with her?"

"Somewhat. We shared a table with the all-knowing Mrs. Daw the other evening."

"The housekeeper?"

"The very one." She tapped her papers together on the desk and then secured them in her arms. "I enjoyed her company very much. I wonder. Would you mind delivering a note from me as well?"

A note from Lady Anneslow might be just the thing to hide his own. "Certainly. I would be happy to oblige."

She sat at another desk, took out a pen and then searched in vain for ink. "Might I share in the well?"

He scooted his chair over and she dipped her pen, scratching a message across the paper. He couldn't begin his own missive until she had quite finished.

"I would love to further our acquaintance. She's just the sort of friend meant for keeping." She stood again, leaving her letter to dry on the top of the desk. "I will leave you to it, then. I'm here myself to choose a title to while away this abysmal weather we are having."

"Thank you again for the paper."

She nodded, an amused glint in her eye and left him alone.

He thought over his words. Did he dare leave this note? Perhaps without his or her name so as not to entrap her. He closed his eyes and thought of her smile, her wit, the beautiful fullness of her mouth. Then he dipped his pen and began to write.

Dear accomplice from the beach,

I hope your time to rest is not too tedious and that you return to the party soon. I have walked by your door too many times to count, wishing every time your prison wardens would give me entrance. But they cannot deny this book.

I have struggled, knowing your plans for romance lie elsewhere, or rather, your plans for marriage lie elsewhere. I doubt very much if romance could ever find you in that "other." But I wonder if perhaps your plans for romance might include me? And I ask, shouldn't romance and marriage be made for each other, as I suspect you and I are? I find myself at a loss without you. When you are well and can accept visitors, I beg an opportunity to court you properly.

Yours. Entirely yours,

Your now highly improper suitor,

Abraham

P.S. Your handkerchief still smells of lemons, and I thank you for it. I shall never return it.

He read through the letter five times before he felt daring enough to send it. What could he lose? She would either accept the idea of his suit or reject him in favor or her original plan with Ridgecrest. He loathed that man more the longer time passed. One thing he most definitely might lose was an opportunity to court Miss Tanning. But the more he thought about her, the calm, practical choice, he could not even fathom such a choice when there was a woman in the world like Lady Felicity. He suspected she was the only woman of her kind, the only one to make him happy. And he couldn't believe he hadn't noticed straight away and spent every waking moment trying to woo her.

He made his way back to the hallway outside her bedroom. As he approached, Mrs. Daw was closing the door.

"Mrs. Daw?"

"Oh, Lord Bolton. I'm sure she will be so very pleased to see you."

His mouth dropped open, amazed at his good fortune. "Might I . . . could I be permitted to see her?"

"Naturally. I will join you so that it is all very proper and on the up and up."

"Oh, I would be most grateful. Is she? Is now a good time?"

"Yes, I think you've come at the perfect time, as she's about ready to revolt in her great boredom."

Mrs. Daw reopened the door and called in. "My lady, you have a visitor."

He peered in over her shoulder, and Lady Felicity's smile warmed him to his toes.

"Oh, please come in, Lord Bolton. I am in great need of diversion. And you are just the man to provide."

Mrs. Daw winked at him. "There now, you see?"

He followed her into the room where she took up a corner seat and pretended not to notice them. Another maid bustled around, and Abraham took up the chair next to Lady Felicity's bed.

The chair sat much lower than the bed. He felt like a boy from the schoolroom in more ways than one. "I brought you something."

She reached for the book. "*Pride and Prejudice*? I've been wanting to read this. How did you know?"

"I don't know. I confess, Mr. Garvey showed me his books and suggested it."

She leafed through the book, stopping on his paper.

"You'll find a note from Lady Anneslowe as well as from myself." He looked over his shoulder at Mrs. Daw who sat with her eyes closed in the corner.

Lady Felicity's eyes widened, and she snapped the book shut.

He shrugged. "Perhaps not entirely improper?"

The same daring spark he'd seen when he met her lit her face. She dipped her head and hugged the book to her chest. "I look forward to reading it."

He stood, wanting more than anything to be closer. Reaching out to clear the hair from her brow, he whispered. "I've missed you. Are you well?"

"Thank you. I am well. They're worried about the cold and the wet, but I should be back with everyone tomorrow."

"With me?"

"If you wish."

"And others?"

Her eyes clouded. "What are you asking?"

"Something I have no right to . . . yet."

She nodded but looked troubled. Then she turned back to him. "I don't know about the others. Some people's company is more preferred than others, but then, preferable company hasn't always been a reason to spend time with another."

He tilted his head. Truer words were never spoken. "While I at one time felt as you do, did you listen to yourself as you spoke just now? Why ever would we choose to spend a lifetime with one not as preferable. It seems foolhardy at best. Consider your words and read your lovely book, and perhaps an infinitely more enjoyable path will open up?"

She nodded, her eyes full of hope. "Perhaps."

He dipped his head and then, before he or Mrs. Daw could stop him, he leaned forward and pressed his lips to her forehead. "Be well, Felicity Honora."

She sucked in her breath. "Thank you."

With one last look, he turned and left the room, winking at Mrs. Daw on the way out.

CHAPTER 12

*A*s soon as Mrs. Daw finished swooning over Lord Bolton and left the room back to her duties, Felicity flipped through the pages to the note, carefully folded inside.

Dear accomplice from the beach,

I hope your time to rest is not too tedious and that you return to the party soon. I have walked by your door too many times to count, wishing every time your prison wardens would give me entrance. But they cannot deny this book.

I have struggled, knowing your plans for romance lie elsewhere, or rather, your plans for marriage lie elsewhere. I doubt very much if romance could ever find you in that other. But I wonder if perhaps your plans for romance might include me? And I ask, shouldn't romance and marriage be made for each other, as I suspect you and I are? I find myself at a loss without you. When you are well and can accept visitors, I beg an opportunity to court you properly.

Yours. Entirely yours,

Your now highly improper suitor,

Abraham

P.S. Your handkerchief still smells of lemons and I thank you for it. I shall never return it.

Her breathing quickened. She'd just received a letter from a man. Instead of being horrified, she felt nothing but an enticing excitement rush through her. She could still feel the pressure, the delicious tingle on her forehead from his lips on her skin. She sunk lower into her bed, hugging the book and letter to her. Then she opened her eyes and read it again.

He wanted to court her, mentioned marriage. She squealed. And then she allowed herself to consider something so delicious as a marriage to the handsome Lord Bolton. She imagined his face, his broad shoulders. She remembered all the funny things he'd said. She laughed out loud. Had she really taught the man needlepoint? She had never taken him seriously, knowing he was a shameless flirt. And yet, he had been serious. And what of Miss Tanning? She didn't know. But here he was declaring his intentions to Felicity.

What would life be like with Lord Bolton? She smiled. Ever so diverting, every day. But then she frowned. And the state of his estate? His brother? Why did he need money so badly? When people discussed Lord Bolton, it was not with the utmost respect, it was more with a smile, an apologetic shrug, and pity. Why?

She sat back in her bed with a frown. Could she give up the chance she had with Lord Ridgecrest to bring her family name back into respectability? If she were to entertain a flirtation with Lord Bolton, if she were to allow his courtship, to test how serious he was, she would lose her chances with Lord Ridgecrest, surely.

A knock at the door surprised her. A maid poked in her head.

"Flowers, my lady."

"Come in." She smiled.

The maid brought in a lovely bouquet of an assortment of flowers she'd seen on her walks in the tall grass along the beach mixed with roses from their garden. "They're lovely."

"It was Lord Ridgecrest that sent them. He said to send his regards."

She pressed her lips together. No secret love notes from him. The staid proper response from Lord Ridgecrest brought her comfort. He was like a rock, unmoving in a great tempest of emotion. She felt sure of her place in society at his side, sure of her family's acceptance, her future children's. He was someone to trust, to rely on. Perhaps. She thought of that moment in the dark hallway where her trust had wavered. But brushed it aside as the normal desires of any man.

Lord Bolton might be exciting and cause her heart to flip, but Lord Ridgecrest was the sensible choice. Her mother had made the exciting choice, but that left things to Felicity to be sensible. As her governess had taught.

She leaned back in her bed again, opening up her book. The letter burned in her memory, but she began reading page one, ignoring its presence a few pages back.

THE WHOLE OF AN AFTERNOON, evening, and morning on the next day passed in a total agony of waiting. Lord Bolton had never felt so anxious for time to pass. And Lord Ridgecrest walked as though he owned the earth. Abraham had never noticed before, but the man competed in everything and felt himself above most others in his presence. And he talked incessantly of the prince. They had announced that Prince George would be joining their party for dinner tomorrow, and Abraham thought the man would start frothing with apoplexy. Ridgecrest couldn't stop discussing the prince, his preferences, his parties, or his connections. The more he talked, the more Abraham wished to shut him up. And that is why he had agreed to participate in the fencing tournament.

He swung his sword in practice, leaping, swishing, lunging. He usually won such tournaments outright, but all he cared about today was beating one man. Once he did that, he'd bow out and go for a ride. Someone needed to show Ridgecrest he wasn't as vastly superior as he thought. As he portended. And that most people did not sit in wonder at all of the words he spoke. Most particularly, he wanted Ridgecrest to realize his own inadequacy at fencing.

He chuckled. He knew he was being childish, but with him and everyone else thinking he had a chance with Lady Felicity, Abraham owed it to himself, if no one else, to show the man a thing or two.

Abraham stepped into the squared-off space. Ridgecrest joined him on the opposite side. They had an audience, a meager one, but Abraham cared only for one. Ridgecrest.

They bowed, touching tips, then stepped away, points out.

Ridgecrest struck out fast and hard.

Abraham matched each blow with a calm ease. There would be time for fast, hard hits.

Ridgecrest worked and lunged and stretched and spun, but Abraham blocked each move as though it were child's play. When he saw an opening, he reached in and tore at the fabric on Ridge-crest's sleeve.

"Stop playing," Ridgecrest said.

"Oh, this is not play."

Ridgecrest scowled and ran at him, pounding with the flat of his sword.

But Abraham blocked every blow. When the man grew too close, Abraham shoved him away with his left hand.

"Stop. Fight."

Abraham bowed.

Ridgecrest ran at him again, and their swords flew at each other, Abraham defending. As Ridgecrest worked harder to conquer, Abraham began his own affront until for every forward thrust of Ridgecrest's, Abraham responded with one of his own. The world whirred in a blur around them, and Abraham concentrated on the conquest right in front of him.

Ridgecrest began to tire, and Abraham thanked his reckless brother for one thing, the countless hours and challenges to fence together.

They circled one way and then back another. Ridgecrest lunged and reached his foot out behind Abraham. He would have tripped backwards, but Abraham caught on to his cheap move and leaped over his leg.

Abraham ripped Ridgecrest's other sleeve and then tore at the fabric at his chest. He danced with ease, the light footwork required to move swiftly, watching Ridgecrest tire further. His hair fell in his flushed face, his costume was a mess, and his eyes were determined and furious.

"You seem as though you have something to prove, Bolton." Ridgecrest's voice was an almost sneer.

"It's just a match in play, Ridgecrest."

He pounded at Bolton in broad, swift strokes. "So you say."

They circled again.

"Is it our mutual lady friend?"

Feminine gasps nearby distracted Abraham, but he kept his eyes firmly on Ridgecrest's hand. "I don't know what you're talking about."

"Some people want to marry without worrying about all the baggage, Bolton. Don't take it too hard. The women will always prefer flirting with you. But one day they will want something more, and that's when they'll come to me."

"I've never seen a woman leave my company for yours."

"Pay attention, Bolton."

Whatever he meant by that, Abraham had had enough. With two swift motions, Ridgecrest was stripped of his sword and had the point of Abraham's at his throat.

"Match."

"Well played, gentlemen."

Abraham barely heard the congratulations or any of the comments around him. He bowed to Ridgecrest and to the room and then turned on his heel and left. Fury pounding through him, he didn't even bother changing, going straight for the stables.

But he stopped at the door. The rain was still pouring down. It would be unwise and cruel to the animals to go for a ride just now.

Still in desperate need to let off some of his pent-up energy and anger, he considered going for a walk in the deluge.

But a soft voice came up behind him. "She loved your visit, hasn't stopped reading the book." Mrs. Daw stood behind him.

He turned, grateful for news of Lady Felicity. "I'm glad. I hoped to brighten what must be a tiresome stay in her room."

"That you did. Much better than the flowers Lord Ridgecrest sent up."

He nodded slowly. "I see."

"She would be appreciating something from the kitchen, perhaps? Or maybe another book? She'll be finishing that one soon enough. I do believe the Garvey's have others by that same author."

He turned and eyed her with new appreciation. "I am in need of an ally."

"I think you will find there are more than one of us who greatly prefers you."

"Excellent. Then I shall go and fetch the titles as you say."

"Wise move. And don't worry. A woman's heart will always control the day, eventually."

He bowed, not totally understanding the problem at hand. Would it be good for him if Lady Felicity's heart won the day? He assumed that's what Mrs. Daw meant. But would she know?

He'd take every suggestion he could get, and right now, he was collecting another book for Lady Felicity. Another book and whatever else she wanted. He was at her command. He knew it, and he hoped she would be gentle with his heart, hoped he could convince her to make them both happy and choose him over anyone else.

CHAPTER 13

*D*ays, weeks, months passed without end all in one afternoon. Actually, she was unsure about the passage of time, but knew that at last she would be leaving her room for dinner this evening and that the celebrated Prince George was purported to have accepted their hosts' invitation to dine with them.

She cared less about Prinny and more about two other gentlemen who would be at the dinner.

She'd all but decided to move forward with her plans for Lord Ridgecrest. But she couldn't resist looking forward to at least seeing Lord Bolton again. When she was with him, she knew everything would turn out all right; she knew she was strong and wise and that she could do whatever she set her mind to. Her interactions with Lord Ridgecrest had even been better when Lord Bolton was involved. And so she couldn't resist more time spent with him, even though it would shortly be coming to a close.

Lord Ridgecrest seemed as dedicated as ever. She had her hopes high that he would be asking for a private audience before the end of the party, perhaps even this very evening. She tried to tell herself that the great pit of darkness that opened at the thought was just nerves. It had to be nerves. Who didn't feel scared about an upcoming proposal? Everyone, she imagined felt nerves.

Her hair was curled to exactness, and her dress fit perfectly. She knew she looked well. And most importantly, she looked proper, as expected.

When she entered the room where guests were gathering before dinner, most smiled in warm welcome. She hadn't come to know all of them very well, but there was a certain camaraderie among guests with such an odd hosting situation. She'd always appreciate Mrs. Garvey. Her care when Felicity was ill could not have been more kind.

Guests lined up to be escorted into dinner, and for a moment, Felicity panicked. When should she enter? It was always by rank, usually dictated by the man's rank, but she would have a place as a lady of title. But no man had come to escort her. Had such a thing been assigned? She always felt so out of place in these situations. Her mother obviously never cared for such details, stubbornly insisting that a person's worth was not dictated by their rank or title.

She almost slipped back out the door in a panic until a deep baritone voice filled her ears and her whole body to her toes with a tingle of expectation. "Lady Felicity."

She curtseyed and placed a hand on his arm. "Lord Bolton. You've come to my rescue, as I was quite unsure when to enter."

"Why, you will come with me. We are to enter shortly, by our mutual friends, the Anslowes."

Relief coursed through her. And with her hand on Lord Bolton's arm, she felt strong. "Is it true? Prince George is coming?"

He dipped his head. "And may I apologize on his behalf for all of the crude and inappropriate things that might leave his mouth in your presence?"

"What . . ."

"Oh, he's terrible. Once he's started imbibing, he only gets worse, carries on, and women are best to decide early on what they would like to be introduced to, so to speak."

Felicity thought about that for a moment, further confusion clouding her judgment. For now that Lord Bolton was at her side, she didn't think she could ever leave him.

They entered, their seats close together, with Lord Bolton at her side and Lord Ridgecrest across from her. He sat at the side of Miss Tanning, and she was thrilled to note that Lady Tinsdale sat on her left. Perhaps dinner would be lovely.

And it was. The food was some of the best she'd ever eaten. Mr. Garvey was present and laughing and entertaining them all. And most fascinating of all, the prince himself sat at the other end of the table. She'd never been in such elevated company, and at first, she felt quite awed by it, but when she noticed that everyone around her acted completely normal and that the prince was nothing but a typical lord, albeit a very jovial one, she relaxed and was able to enjoy the conversation around her.

Lord Ridgecrest smiled across the table at her. "I'm pleased you are well."

Miss Tanning leaned toward her. "Yes, I heard it was quite dreadful, caught in the middle of a rainstorm. Was it?"

"I've never felt so cold. The clouds rolled in without me even realizing."

Mr. Garvey called down to their end of the table. "I, too, am pleased you are well."

Mortified to be the very center of attention, the prince himself looking her way, she cleared her throat. "Yes, thank you. Mrs. Garvey was the most attentive of hostesses. I imagine I owe my recovery to her."

"And to some lovely gifts from one particular suitor, if I may say so." Mr. Garvey laughed, overly loud.

"Oh ho!" The prince raised his glass to her, which meant everyone else followed suit. "Do I detect a blush? Who is this woman's suitor?"

"I'm sure I don't know, Your Highness." She dipped her head, mortified. Lord Bolton grunted beside her.

The prince called out. "You don't know? Oh, that's a lesson for you, young man. Your targeted love doesn't even know." He roared out an overly loud laugh. "Not very good at it, is he? If she doesn't even know?"

Others joined him, but the group closest to her remained silent. She daren't look at anyone, her hands tightly wound together in her lap.

"Oh dear," Mrs. Dotting muttered from her place on the other side of Miss Tinsdale.

Mr. Garvey laughed. "Come now, Ridgecrest, best fess up. No need to leave your lady waiting."

Felicity's gaze whipped up to Lord Ridgecrest. She felt and saw Lord Bolton stiffen beside her.

Lord Ridgecrest's face drained of color, and then he licked his lips. "I'm not sure to what you are referring. If you are alluding to some claim I might have on the young woman, you are gravely mistaken. We move in different spheres. I could never lower myself to an alliance with such a family. We are friends, a long standing debt to be paid, nothing more."

Felicity gasped, as did several other ladies at the table. But instead of cowering away from his overly rude rejection, she felt a fire burn inside, an indignation so strong she fisted her hands and was about to give him the reprimand of her life when Lord Bolton rested his hand over hers.

He tilted his head. "Did I hear you correctly? Do you feel yourself above Lady Felicity?"

"Oh, don't get your sensibilities all in a flutter, Lord Bolton. If you understood the circumstances—"

"I understand perfectly well. What I see is a woman twice your equal in every way. I see an honorable soul. Felicity Honora Felicity comes from the oldest of family lines on her father's side. Titled. But she is your superior in every other way imaginable as well. Where you are the appearance of goodness, she is good. Where you are the appearance of respectability, she knows what it means to represent her class. Where you are wealthy and titled, she is wealthy, titled, and sharing. Where you lack, she excels. If there is to be any lowering in an alliance with Lady Felicity and you"—his mouth turned in disgust—"the lowering would all be one sided. Yours."

The table was silent. Everyone stared at Lord Bolton. Felicity could not take her eyes off him. She gushed out her held breath. "Thank you."

He seemed unable to find his speech, but nodded to her. "I meant every word."

The prince began to clap, and everyone else followed suit. "I have never heard such a brilliant declaration. I feel by those standards, we would all be marrying up in such an alliance with the perfect Lady Felicity."

Lord Ridgecrest snorted, but the warning look from Lord Bolton quieted him immediately. Lady Felicity reached over under the table and laced her fingers with Lord Bolton's.

"It seems to me, Mr. Garvey, you chose the wrong man when you called out her suitor."

"Quite right, Your Highness."

Thankfully, that ended interference from the prince or their host. Felicity daren't look at Lord Ridgecrest, or anyone else, but her gaze clung to Lord Bolton as the lifeline he was. "You didn't need to do that."

"I couldn't help myself." His gaze flicked to Lord Ridgecrest and his eyes narrowed, but when he turned back to her, they softened, and Felicity couldn't believe she'd ever desired another. "Might I request an audience with you later? Privately?"

"Wouldn't such a thing be improper?"

"Decidedly."

"Then most certainly."

His grin started small but grew as to overtake his face. She laughed. And he joined her. But she did not let go of his hand, instead choosing to eat the entirety of her meal with her left hand.

CHAPTER 14

*A*braham paced in the library, by himself. Lady Felicity had agreed to meet him that evening, but it was past the time of their designation. He had begun to wear his path, so he turned to find a seat by the fire. As soon as he sat, the door moved open. He sprung to his feet.

Lady Felicity entered, her eyes wide, her feet moving slowly, and Abraham wasn't sure what to make of her. But he grinned in welcome and held out his hand. "You came."

"I almost scared myself out of it."

"Oh, but why would you do such a thing? There is only happiness where we are concerned."

She stepped closer. "And that is what convinced me to keep our appointment. With you, I am always happy."

"Precisely my thoughts on the matter of you and I." He reached for her hand. "Although, I'm so unaccountably sad and rightfully angry at Lord Ridgecrest for his insolence."

She shook her head. "Do not be concerned. He has his reasons. My mother—"

"It matters not to me whatever you might say regarding your mother. I meant what I said to the room at large. And I feel equally inadequate in your presence as any other should."

"You are too good to me." She shook her head. "You must know. My mother's family, my money even, comes from trade . . ."

He waited for her to say more. When she was silent, wide-eyed and fearsome, he laughed. "This is it? This is the great lack of respect of your family?"

"Well, doesn't it matter?"

"Not to me." He shook his head. "I'm just relieved you have some money, for that is all we will have to live upon, I'm afraid. My brother has spent it all, wasted at the tables and other riotous living. So you see, where your familial associations are now only honorable, they will be less so were you to align yourself with the Boltons."

"But you have behaved honorably."

"I have."

"Then I, too, am marrying above myself in you."

"What a pair we make for each other."

She reached in a reticule and pulled out a folded piece of paper.

"Where did you find such a thing as paper in this house?"

CHARMED BY HIS LORDSHIP

"As I'm sure you know, it wasn't easy." She opened it. "But it is a letter I wrote you."

Abraham clapped his hands. "Oh, this is delicious. Let's sit by the fire and enjoy this moment of Felicity's greatest disrepute."

"Do you know, I don't even feel ashamed?"

"And why should you?"

She shrugged. They sat together, Abraham as close as he could sit to her. She patted his hand. "Now, listen."

"Dear Abraham." She gasped, her hand to her mouth. "Abraham." After searching his face and he in great amusement nodding his acceptance of the use of his first name.

"Dear Abraham—"

"Yes, I know the beginning, but what follows?" He chuckled. "Or is that it? You couldn't get past my name?"

"Oh hush. There's more. Perhaps I should just let you read it?"

"May I?"

She paused, watching his face. "No, I shall."

He groaned.

"I can. I promise." She cleared her throat again.

"Dear Abraham—"

"If I didn't love the sound of my name on your lips so much, I would complain more."

She held up a hand. *"It is with great happiness that I write you this letter. For I have come to recognize in myself an affection so great I hardly know what to do with my feelings. For they overflow into every-*

thing I am attempting to accomplish. I can hardly sit for my maid's ministrations. Even needlepoint lacks meaning."

He gasped appropriately, which made her laugh.

"For the longest time I thought these growing feelings were to be discounted, ignored to be replaced by thoughts of the more responsible choice, that giving in to these aching desires would be akin to the sins of my mother. But now I realize how very wrong I've been. My mother made the highest and best choice. And like her, I want to be with the man I love.

"But I'd like to be clear: in doing so, I am not choosing less of a man. In choosing the man that I love, I am also choosing the very best of men. One who is kind, and giving, and fun and respectable in every way but more than all of that, an honorable man who is deserving of my love forever.

"With great love and affection,

"Your Felicity Honora Honeyfield."

She wiped at her tears and Abraham reached for the paper. "May I?"

"What?"

"Keep it. Of course."

"Yes."

He folded it carefully and placed it in his jacket pocket, and then he lifted her to her feet. "And now my dear, precious, Felicity."

"Could I make a request?"

"Anything."

"The name I prefer above all others is Honora."

"Is it?"

"Yes."

He pulled her closer and placed a hand at the side of her face. "Then Honora."

She shivered.

"There are a few things I'd like to discuss with you."

She nodded back, eyes shining.

He studied her face, her beautiful, innocent, caring face, and he was swept away. "I love you, Honora. I want you in my life all my days, as my dearest companion, the wife at my side."

She smiled up at him, leaning into his palm. "I love you too, Abraham. That would make me the happiest I could ever imagine."

He sat her back down and kneeled in front of her. His precious lady. "Honora, will you do me the incredible honor of allowing me to be your husband?"

She reached out her hand, tentatively, carefully, and touched his hair, swirling it in a curl around her finger. Then she ran a hand down the side of his face, her finger trailing along his bottom lip. She lowered her hand to his chest and rested it, as before, right over his heartbeat. Then she lifted his hand to place over her heart. Her face filled with wonder, she whispered, "Can this be so?"

"Yes, my darling. Now, please, will you answer the question?"

"Oh. My, of course. Yes. Yes, yes. Most certainly yes. I will marry you and be the happiest person on this whole of England, I'm certain."

He picked her up and swung her in a circle, then brought her close, wrapping his arms around her back. He searched her face.

She lifted her chin. Her lips were full, soft looking, slightly parted.

He could wait no longer. He lowered his mouth to hers, pulling her closer. He searched her eyes, and then the pull of her hands rose to the back of his neck, and their gentle insistent tugging made him smile. She stood on tip-toes, reaching for him.

He happily obliged and was lost to her soft mouth, exploring, pressing, loving this woman who had agreed to be his.

She pressed her teeth on his lip, which brought every feeling to a heightened expression. Her hand rested on his chest. He covered it with his own and rested his head against hers. Her soft sigh made him smile. Then he tugged her by the hand out the door. "I'll walk you to your room."

"I suppose that would be wise."

"And proper."

CHAPTER 15

*T*he days passed in a whirl. Felicity supposed that the party continued around them. She tried to be happy for Miss Tanning and Lord Ridgecrest, who declared their engagement shortly after she and Lord Bolton had announced the same. A hot air balloon ride, dinners, parlor games, even a grand ball at the end where she was forced to dance with others in attendance besides her precious Abraham, all flew past her in memory, but none of it seemed to matter expect that her Abraham was there at her side.

When the last day had arrived and all their luggage was packed into Felicity's carriage, Abraham rode up on his horse. "If you get too lonely in there, just wave your hand and Mrs. Dotting and I will trade places."

She laughed at Mrs. Dotting's horrified exclamations.

They were on their way to her childhood home, to Haversham, where he would speak to her father.

As she thought about leaving this house party, she felt a pang of sadness her mother would never know Abraham and a tinge of regret she'd not come to understand or appreciate her mother until long after she had passed.

But a part of her hoped, guessed that perhaps she was near. Just in case, she called out on the wind, "Thank you, Mother."

Abraham rode up beside her. "Miss me already?"

"Of course."

He reached his hand out and grasped at her outstretched fingers. "I love you."

"I love you too."

THE END

FOLLOW JEN

Jen has five other published books

The Nobleman's Daughter
Two lovers in disguise

Scarlet
The Pimpernel retold

Spun of Gold
Rumplestilskin Retold

Dating the Duke
Time Travel: Regency man in NYC

Tabitha's Folly
Four over protective Brothers

To read Damen's Secret

The Villain's Romance

Follow her Newsletter

Read on for Chapter ONE of our next book in the Havencrest series.

Interested in our previous House Party books? Read on for sneak peeks into the other Regency House Party Series—

.

THE CAPTAIN'S LADY

Chapter One

Lucy Brook was breathless as she fairly flew towards the bank. Between the yeasty smell from Offley's tavern and the oppressive summer heat, she needed a drink of water and a fan.

"How long ago did Captain Sharpe arrive?" she asked her accountant.

Mr. Nicolson kept pace beside her, his long-legged stride eating up the distance. "A quarter of an hour, perhaps. I left to find you the moment he stepped foot inside."

"Did he state his business?"

"No. But he has a new secretary."

Her stomach constricted around the kippers she had eaten for her morning meal. Lucy hoped she wasn't too late, but she didn't know what to expect. Captain Sharpe had always corresponded by letter, never in person. She feared the damage the latest newspaper articles could do. Carriage wheels clacked over the narrow cobble-stone of Henrietta Street. The shops presented a solid front—no break in the ranks, no alley or crack, not even to let in a breeze. London in July was stifling.

Breathing heavily, they arrived at Number 27, Tilney's Bank. Mr. Nicolson opened the heavy door for her. This bank was like home with its comforting scents of paper and ink.

"Everything will work out," she told herself. She lifted her chin and stiffened her spine, scanning for the captain. Though they had never been introduced, she had seen him on a rainy day when she was riding in Hyde Park. He was on foot, and even if she had not almost run him over, it had been hard not to gawk at him. His wet uniform had pulled against broad shoulders, and when he lifted somber eyes and smiled tentatively, revealing white teeth against sun-bronzed skin, words had fled her. She would recognize him the moment she saw him.

She stood on her tiptoes to scan the bank's entry for Captain Sharpe. Everyone seemed to turn their direction—from the tellers, loan officers, and customers, to the actress sitting on one of the cushioned chairs. A gentleman stared openly at her over the folded edge of his newspaper.

Lucy's already-warm face blazed. She clasped her hands together and dropped her head, unable to meet anyone's gaze.

"Did *The Times* print something new about my inheritance?" she whispered to Mr. Nicolson.

Mr. Nicolson shrugged.

Lucy squared her shoulders and walked through the lobby in a straight course to the bank manager's office. Perhaps Captain Sharpe was still here. Surely the bank manager had delayed him until she arrived. Perhaps the captain's business today was of no importance.

The office door was closed but raised voices carried. Her breath hitched and she glanced at Mr. Nicolson. The meeting was underway and it didn't seem to be going well. Lucy smoothed the wisps of hair escaping her chignon. When she crossed the threshold, she would sink into her favorite chair, push the peculiar tension from her, and face whatever came with confidence. Her late Grandfather Tilney had bequeathed her Tilney's Bank, and she would prove herself capable.

Mr. Nicolson pushed his spectacles on his nose. "Are you ready?"

No. "Yes."

Mr. Nicolson cracked open the door. There was no waiting on ceremony today.

Her brother-in-law, Reuben Hardy, pushed his large frame to his feet and waved them in. "Miss Brook. Mr. Nicolson." His booming bass voice welcomed them.

Besides Reuben, there was only one other man present, and he was not the captain. Lucy frowned. Was she too late? Had Captain Sharpe left already? She had half a mind to go find the captain, to chase him down and ask him outright. But perhaps his presence at the bank wasn't so unaccountable.

Reuben cleared his throat and gestured with a beefy hand. "Miss Brook, may I introduce Mr. Keats, the secretary for one of our most important clients, Captain Jack Sharpe."

She curtseyed. "It's a pleasure to meet you, Mr. Keats."

Mr. Keats sniffed and gave the barest of bows. He kept his chin unusually high, despite having almost none. He looked her over, one pale thin eyebrow rising into his limp hair, a look of consternation on his face, as if puzzling the window and glass tax for Tilney's.

Lucy wound the strap of her reticule around her hand. *He is only a solicitor,* she reminded herself. *He may think he's in charge, but he holds no more power than an animal at the Royal Menagerie.*

Mr. Nicolson held out a velvet chair for Lucy, and she perched on the end of it, swallowing her discomfort. She removed her gloves to grasp the armrests of her grandfather's chair, and the tangible connection to him brought a lump to her throat.

"Would you give me a brief summary of your meeting with Mr. Keats so far?" she asked, discreetly wiping at the beads of sweat on her forehead.

"Of course," Reuben said. "First, can I offer you a drink?"

"Yes—" Lucy said in the same moment Mr. Keats answered, "No."

She and Mr. Keats eyed one another a second time.

"My business here is concluding, and I do not wish to restate it," Mr. Keats said.

"Since it concerns Miss Brook, we will take our time to restate our business thus far." Reuben's tone held censure.

Mr. Keats murmured, "I've never discussed business with a lady."

His comment pushed on a bruise, but Lucy kept her face serene. She accepted the glass of water from Reuben and tried to sip slowly, even though she was parched. Reuben might have hair sticking up in the back and a permanently rumpled cravat around his thick neck, but he also had the warm brown eyes of a beloved dog. And a loyal streak Lucy admired. She was proud to call him her brother-in-law, though they kept their relationship formal at the bank.

The men settled back in their seats, Reuben and Mr. Nicolson flanking her, and the pale and pinched Mr. Keats directly across. Even with the support, Lucy could not be lulled into believing she was safe.

"Let me fill you in," Reuben began. "Captain Sharpe arrived and introduced his new secretary, Mr. Keats, who will be conducting his business." He paused, and his brows knit. "The captain wishes to withdraw the entirety of his assets and transfer them to another bank."

Lucy's mouth opened, her throat going dry. Her mind whirled, calculating the numbers, the probabilities, and difficulties involved in shoring up liquidity with such a substantial transfer.

"*All* of his assets?" she clarified. "This seems sudden. If we can understand Captain Sharpe's needs, what his concerns are, I'm confident we—"

"I advised my client to proceed at once," Mr. Keats interrupted.

"You told him to?" Her body locked in place.

"Yes." Mr. Keats's small chin tipped in the semblance of a smile.

Reuben placed an elbow on the desk, leaning into Lucy's line of fire. "Captain Sharpe has been a loyal customer at Tilney's Bank since he first became an officer. We have always taken care of his interests."

Mr. Keats spared him a glance. "I have stated Captain Sharpe's desires clearly."

Had he? She couldn't let this account go. Other patrons might follow his example, since the captain was a prominent figure, even if he wasn't in society much. She could only begin to guess how the loss of the captain's finances would affect the bank's assets and stability. Most patrons with a fortune as large as his used multiple banks, but the captain used only one. Hers.

"You have mentioned no complaints," Lucy began. "Is another bank offering a higher rate of return? Has Tilney's failed Captain Sharpe in providing service? If you share the plain and practical reasons, we may be able to resolve the matter without you needing to go to such great lengths."

Mr. Keats's gaze locked on hers, and his pale eyes flashed with something dark. "Miss Brook, you are precisely the reason. You may have inherited this bank, but you should not attempt to meddle in matters so complex."

The burst of contention hit her with palpable force, knocking her stomach inside out. She leaned against the back of her grandfather's chair.

Mr. Keats's bony index finger jabbed the table as he spoke. "Banking is no place for a woman. It is unbecoming for a lady."

"That is enough," Reuben warned.

Lucy felt as if Mr. Keats had slapped her. Heat exploded in her face and radiated through her body. Even her fingers tingled. "That's absurd." She was a lady and longed for everything a woman of her age wished for—a husband and children. But personal aches could not sidetrack her now. The bank's success mattered most.

"You may have inherited your grandfather's bank, but a woman should leave the running of it to the manager and the board of trustees," he said, his voice patronizing. "It weakens my . . . my client's confidence in Tilney's as a sound financial institution. So, as advised, Captain Sharpe shall withdraw the entirety of his funds."

She had owned the bank for a mere year and was already losing Tilney's foremost customer.

All voices seemed to erupt at once. All except for hers. She sat mute.

Mr. Nicolson's narrow shoulders bunched. "Look at our financial reports. We rival the Bank of England for organization and guaranteed payments. How is that for confidence?"

"You expect us to hand over his assets in one afternoon? It takes time," Reuben boomed.

Mr. Keats stood. "Gentlemen." Splotchy red crept up his face and into his thinning hair. "Gentlemen," he said again, as if Lucy were invisible. Perhaps she was. "I give you a fortnight's notice. Captain Sharpe is on holiday in Brighton until the fourteenth. You have until then to make the arrangements. I will send you the particulars on when we will meet again." He snapped his leather case closed with finality. "I bid you good day." He swung the door shut with a resounding bang.

Lucy covered her face with her hands. What would cause Captain Sharpe to lose confidence in Tilney's Bank? Was she really so inept?

In the stillness, Reuben shuffled his feet by the closed door. "We have the funds. We can remain solvent even with this blow."

She glanced up at the two men she trusted. "Captain Sharpe is an influential man. What if another customer follows suit? And then another? It could spell disaster." Sweat trickled down her spine.

"Fiend seize it. This is because of the rubbish *The Times* printed this morning," Mr. Nicolson said.

Lucy snatched the discarded newspaper on the table.

"Page three," Reuben said, taking the chair across from her.

She smoothed a finger over the wrinkled column. It was titled "Bank Heiress Going Bankrupt." Her heart sank like a paperweight. Why must people assume she was incapable of intelligent thoughts?

"This article makes me out to be a light-headed peagoose." She tried to swallow past the sting of unshed tears. "No wonder Mr. Keats lost confidence in Tilney's. Who else will leave based on this?"

"Captain Sharpe is only one customer," Reuben said.

"One wealthy and influential customer." No one else had invested such a large amount of money at Tilney's. She pressed a hand to the twinge in her chest.

"So you wear a dress. I don't understand what all the hum is about." Mr. Nicolson adjusted his spectacles. "Two other women own thriving banks in London."

"Yes, but Mrs. Coutts has the Prince Regent as a customer." Reuben drummed his fingers on the table. "And Lady Jersey is . . . well, Lady Jersey, a patroness of Almack's. Perceptions are hard to change."

Lucy swallowed. "Which is why we need Captain Sharpe to remain a customer at Tilney's. I have no clout in society. *The Times* made my faults abundantly clear."

Lucy wondered, for the hundredth time, why her grandfather had entrusted his life's work to her rather than a male relative. Surely he had anticipated the obstacles?

"Some underestimate you, but don't believe them," Reuben soothed. "*The Times* misrepresented the facts. Everyone at Tilney's saw your commitment as your grandfather's health declined. Besides you are a senior partner." His raised his eyebrows. "Lucy, he choose his heir carefully. He praised you for your quick mind and forceful nature."

Lucy nodded, her chin trembling. Only her grandfather would praise her for a forceful nature. She had not been forceful during Mr. Keats' tirade.

"Miss Brook, only a fool would think you could single-handedly destroy Tilney's," Mr. Nicolson said with a warm smile.

Lucy smiled and clasped her trembling hands. "You are right. We can work together to figure this out. Mr. Keats has strong opinions." She blew out a breath and centered her thoughts. "This is my question now: is Captain Sharpe in full agreement, or is his secretary leading this?"

Reuben tilted his head. "There is one way to find out. Mr. Keats shared the details of Captain Sharpe's trip to Brighton—and the lofty connections at a house party at the Garvey's."

Lucy lifted her head, her heart lifting. "That's it. I will go to Brighton and speak with Captain Sharpe." Hope rose inside her.

Mr. Nicolson glanced from Reuben to Lucy, then held up his hand. "Just a moment. What is this about the Garveys? And how do you propose to meet Captain Sharpe if he is invited and you are not?"

"I happen to know Mr. Garvey," Reuben said with a grin. "He's a bit of a dandy, even at his age, but a clever old chap. He spends time with the Prince Regent. Not my usual company. Each summer he hosts a large house party at Havencrest, his estate in Brighton."

"Can you obtain an invitation?" Lucy held her breath.

Reuben rubbed his jaw and nodded. "I believe so. Mr. Garvey is generous and enjoys company. I'll send a letter immediately, and since Brighton is only a short distance, we should receive word before nightfall."

Lucy stood. "We need Captain Sharpe's holdings and his show of confidence." Captain Sharpe's prize money was a hefty sum. Likely two hundred times his annual salary as a naval captain. "If you procure an invitation, then I am willing to do anything to win him over."

"Win over? What do you intend to do?" Mr. Nicolson eyed her in a way that made her stomach turn. "The other two women bankers *are* married. Getting married would add credibility to your role."

Her face heated. "I hold no foolish romantic notions. Do you think I have marriage proposals to choose from?"

The idea was ludicrous. Fortune hunters and dandies abounded, but unaffected gentlemen did not. Besides, even if her heart sometimes longed for more, her mind knew better. She alone directed her life, and she enjoyed that control. A husband would limit her, wouldn't he?

"You're in mourning. No gentleman would seek to court you while in mourning," Reuben said.

"Well, Brighton will be strictly for business," she stated firmly.

"It is none of my concern. Forgive me for being a dunderhead." Mr. Nicolson grimaced.

Lucy relaxed her posture. He was like a brother to her and she couldn't help teasing him to prod him out of his guilt. "No one who can greet every client by name even after one meeting and can balance investments books is a dunderhead. You dolt."

Mr. Nicolson smiled, and Lucy laughed.

"Suitors or not, you do need a proper chaperone, Lucy. You know your sister would love to escort you." Reuben smiled kindly.

"Even with little Thomas?" Lucy didn't mean to intrude, but he was a year and a half old, and her sister had not fully regained her energy.

"Perhaps I should attend as well," Reuben hedged, his brows drawn.

"That is a fine idea. And I would be grateful to you both," she encouraged. Reuben worked long hours at the bank. He might enjoy a holiday. She couldn't recall a time when he wasn't buried in paperwork. "Such short notice will be disruptive. If Charlotte cannot be separated from Thomas, then please encourage her to bring him. You know I adore him." Perhaps the trip would jolly Charlotte out of her melancholy.

"I can manage things here, Miss Brook," Mr. Nicolson volunteered. "And I am on call for a quick ride to Brighton, if I am needed."

"How do you plan on approaching this issue with Captain Sharpe?" Reuben asked.

Lucy rubbed her hands together and cast her eyes over the ledgers and books. "Surely he will change his mind once he sees our bank's holdings and securities."

"That is your plan?" Mr. Nicolson's eyes rounded.

Lucy frowned. "What more is there?"

Reuben drummed his fingers on the mahogany desk. "I have some advice for you, Miss Brook. Please take this in the spirit it is meant." He cleared his throat. "After listening to Mr. Keats' concerns, I suggest you treat a meeting with Captain Sharpe as a social call. Make his acquaintance. Meet him on agreeable terms as a friend among his friends. I am sure he will see your levelheadedness and form his own opinion about you, which we can then build on."

The image of Captain Sharpe came to mind, his piercing eyes and a presence larger than life. Lucy narrowed her eyes, trying to picture herself relating to him without the structure of her position at the bank. A longing for companionship stirred like dust best left undisturbed.

"A social call. I agree." Mr. Nicolson tilted his head and gestured to her hair. "You should try arranging your hair differently. One of the new styles."

She refused the desire to smooth her hair.

"Ringlets, and maybe a few ornaments, too." He turned towards Reuben for confirmation.

"If you know so much, then you should attend as my lady's maid," Lucy quipped.

"I am holding down the castle here, remember?"

Reuben rubbed his chin. "Yes, you've been in half-mourning long enough." He warmed to the topic. "How about one of those dresses the young ladies wear with the . . . the flounces." His thick fingers traced a path on his beefy upper arm.

Lucy raised an eyebrow and laughed at these men giving her advice on her appearance. "I suppose I have stayed in mourning longer than needed." She had been especially close to her grandfather. The grief of losing him still shrouded her in a fog some days, but it was time to move on to sunnier places.

"Purple makes your complexion look a little sickly," Mr. Nicolson said.

"I do not wear purple. I wear lavender," she huffed. True, lavender was not her best color. She preferred lilac with its pink undertone for her complexion. Still, she understood the clumsy message. "I will see what I can do to freshen my look."

"Your only worry is to make a good impression," Reuben said.

Lucy placed a hand to her forehead. "There is so much to do." She should air out her gowns from last season. She needed to inform her maid. And she must help Charlotte prepare as well.

Reuben opened a bottle of ink. "I will figure out a way to broach the subject of the captain's financial concerns. Go pack, and I'll leave as soon as I send a note."

Gratitude formed a lump in her throat. "Let us hope this works." It was a broken prayer and a desperate hope.

To read the rest of The Captain's Lady, click HERE.

TABITHA'S FOLLY: SHOCKING PROPOSITION

*N*o one saw Tabitha standing in the doorway of her brother, Tauney's, room.

James, the valet, lifted clothes *out* of Tauney's trunks in large stacks instead of loading them *in*. Neat, color-coordinated piles of breeches and jackets decorated the bedding, and Tabitha's worry increased.

She shook her head. "We are already so late."

Tauney, only nine months her elder, finished giving animated instructions to James and then waved his hand in her direction. "Late. Psht. The party doesn't even begin for two days."

Of course he would refuse to understand. As the only girl in a family of four brothers, and his closest sibling, she felt responsible for him. She tried another tactic. "If we don't leave now, we will have to delay our journey an extra day and stay at a local inn."

The valet rushed past them, at last packing clothing into Tauney's trunks.

"The local inns. How dreadful." Tauney grimaced. "Do you remember the last time we stayed in one?" His face was so comical, his mouth twisted in disgust. Tabitha couldn't help but laugh.

"But that is exactly my point, though it wasn't so bad."

"For you. My valet had to sleep in the barn. He wasn't even presentable when he came to help me get ready in the morning." His voice lowered to a whisper. "He flicked hay off his person"—Tauney shuddered—"in my presence. It fell to the floor by my foot, and I had to train one eye on it while dressing so as to rid my room of it later." He leaned closer. "Didn't want to hurt his feelings. Good valets are difficult to find, you know."

She often felt pity for his valet.

Her brother was of the opinion that since women spent so many hours concerned with their appearances, they would appreciate the same from men.

Tabitha couldn't argue with that sentiment, especially if they smelled nice. The memory of a distinct earthy aroma warmed her. And she wondered if *he* had arrived. She turned to hide her blush.

She hurried down the stairs. If they were to avoid a war like Napoleon had never seen, she would need to make excuses for Tauney to her other brothers.

The balls on the billiards table cracked and rolled, making her smile. Memories of many a Christmas when their father was still alive, teaching the young Eastons how to play pool, brought a comforting sense of family and home.

She had three of the best men of the *ton* standing right here in her study. And one upstairs, who sometimes had feathers for brains.

"Well, where is he?" Edward, the eldest, frowned.

She laughed, "He has decided on a new color scheme."

When the others groaned, she held up her hand, "But he has promised he is almost finished. I have to admit I am a bit excited to see what he and James accomplish."

"Well I most certainly am not." Edward's frown deepened. "We promised the countess not to be late. She asked for our particular assistance in helping some of the ladies feel welcome."

Julian humphed. "Of course she did. Trying to hitch us to a woman like all the other mothers in the *ton*. If it wasn't for you, little sister, I would have stayed far away from this house party." As handsome as Julian was, with many women vying for his hand, he naturally felt a bit stifled.

She could well understand the sentiment.

"Come now man, the hunt." Oscar, the fun-loving Corinthian of the bunch, grinned. "You have yet to best me in the hunt." He eyed his next shot. "This will not be the year of course." He sent another ball in a blur across the table and then raised an eyebrow. "But I would think you'd be anxious to try."

Julian took his turn, knocking in all four of the balls. With a satisfied grin, he said,

"This is the year, dear brother."

"Ha-Ha!" Tabitha loved it when they puffed and bristled in fun. "Shall I make a wager?" She won all sorts of money from her brothers, especially when they were pitted against each other.

Julian laughed. "A wager she says! If the matrons could hear you now!"

"We've corrupted her." Edward's eyes held warmth, and she knew a part of him was secretly pleased. "I knew it would happen. What diamond talks as you do?"

Oscar, ever positive, added, "And yet she is a diamond. The books at Whites are filled with their own wagers as to who will win her hand."

Every brother's face went ashen.

She blushed. "It's not as if there is anything to worry about..." But how embarrassing to be discussed in such a manner.

Edward looked positively ill, loosening his cravat, and she began to wonder what had them so concerned.

"What could possibly go wrong?" She looked from face to face. A new sense of foreboding began in the back of her throat in a particular, pointed tightness.

After a silence no one filled, Edward finally said, "It wouldn't hurt for each of you brothers to be looking for wives as well, wealthy ones."

Julian pounded his brother's back. "Always the responsible one." Then he turned to Tabitha. "You are the one we need to focus on this year, Tabby Cat."

"Well, it certainly won't help if you go around addressing me like that."

"Why not? Your *endearing* nickname hasn't turned Henry away."

"Turned me away from what?"

Tabitha's stomach flipped, and she whirled around to face the sixth member of their party.

With a sharp chiseled jawline and eyes sparkling in amusement, Henry filled the doorway. As a dear family friend, most of her childhood memories included Henry. But every time she saw him, a nervous energy coursed through her. She grinned up at him in welcome, but he was looking at Julian.

The brother with the honor of Henry's attention jabbed a thumb in her direction. "Tabby thinks her nickname might not be the thing." He winked.

She dipped her head to hide the blush. "Henry's opinion doesn't count."

"Ho, Ho!" Julian nudged him. "Do you hear that? You don't count."

Henry winked at her. "I suppose she means because I am like a brother? Always present, even when you don't want me." His warm eyes twinkled at her.

She shrugged, looking away. *He will never see. How can I make him see?*

Julian shoved him playfully. "You've heard it often enough, and yet here you are."

"Glutton for punishment." He snatched away the stick and took a turn hitting a ball across the table. "And who says I am here for Tabby? Cook's meat pie can't be beat in any house."

She lifted her chin, suddenly defiant. "Besides, I have no desire to be married."

Laughter filled the room.

"Tabitha Easton, on the shelf."

Oscar shook his head. "That'll never happen."

But Edward moved closer to her, concern on his face. "Ever?"

She sat in the nearest chair. "I suppose it will be a wonderful pastime someday."

"Pastime, she says. *Pastime.*" Julian shook his head. "Let me tell you dear sister. Marriage is like a gentle lead on a new mare. At first she likes the feel. It's soft and nice, appears harmless. But then it pulls tighter and tighter until *ack!*" He demonstrated a noose around the throat with his hands. "It cinches so tight you cannot break away."

A part of her tightened inside like that rope; she wasn't sure why.

Henry cleared his throat, bent down beside her chair, and put his arm across her shoulders.

She felt her neck heat and turned to him, searching his eyes, inches from her own. His expression was playful and full of warmth. She could barely breathe and forced herself to swallow.

"Come now, it isn't as bad as all that." Henry's eyes turned tender. "Let's not ruin it for her."

Before she could stop herself, she leaned closer.

His voice, like a warm breeze, circled around and tickled her insides. "Marriage would be wonderful to the right person, someone to share the thoughts you tell no one else. Your closest friend..."

She smiled and closed her eyes. *Friend.* Would he want such a thing with her? They were friends. Perhaps he was considering it. As she searched his face, nothing seemed different, and yet, there was a new sparkle in his eyes. She grinned in response.

Then the brothers burst into laughter, and her irritation rose. She stood to leave.

Julian rested a hand on Henry's shoulder. "Is that what you do with the women, Henry? Bare your innermost thoughts?"

Oscar looked perplexed. "I don't have innermost thoughts."

"None of us do." Julian's eyes held the tears of laughter. "No wonder Henry can't hang onto a woman."

Tabitha turned in the doorway. "Well, I thought it lovely." She tried to show support as her eyes met Henry's.

His wink sent her insides flipping in funny circles, and she placed a hand on her stomach.

He returned to the table taking a hit at the nearest of three balls, the game forgotten by the others. "Of course she thinks it's lovely, being a woman. I don't expect the rest of your sorry selves to understand."

Oscar snatched the stick. "Whoa there, our sister is not a woman."

Julian laughed. "Oh yes she is! Have you seen her lately?"

She wished to hide beneath the floorboards. And felt so lonely for a sister it nearly caused pain. Ever since her mother had taken ill, she had precious few moments with anyone female she could trust.

"Well, we best get used to the idea." Oscar held up one finger. "Because all the men at this house party are going to notice."

Henry nodded. "Especially when she wears green."

Her face blazed, and she couldn't take any more. "I am right here, you know."

"Then you get to listen in." Edward waved a hand in her direction. "This conversation doesn't require your participation."

Indignation rose. And a great pit of fear opened. Could they have no care for her thoughts?

Oscar stood taller. "Yes. We will review the strategies to keep you protected when we arrive. Only the very worthy shall get past us."

Henry cleared his throat. "Have we decided who she is to marry?"

Tabitha trembled to hear that question spoken so carelessly by his lips. "I believe that

decision is mine." Her voice cracked. She rested a hand on Edward's arm. "These choices are best left in the hands of those they most affect."

Her eldest brother did have sympathy in his eyes, but he said, "It's not really your decision. Father left me in charge of your welfare and wrote in his will how I was to go about ensuring a good and productive marriage arrangement for you."

"We will consider your opinion, of course." Julian's calm tones lessened her mounting discomfort. "But we are all attending this infernal party because we need reinforcements to keep the leeches away."

"Leeches?" This party was sounding more dreadful every moment.

Julian grimaced. "Yes, those undesirables who seek fortune."

Oscar chimed in. "Or that we don't like."

"Or have any sniveling habits. Or can't play cards worth—"

"Or don't know how to hunt a fox." Henry added, moving to stand beside her again.

She loved the surge of tingles that shot through her, as much as she wanted to slink away and hide from them.

"Or any who enjoy battledore." Oscar's calculating expression increased Tabitha's irritation.

They all stopped. Edward asked, "What's wrong with battledore?"

"Oh nothing. I just can't have anyone being overly good at it and beat me at all the family gatherings."

Julian squinted, considering. "You've hit upon something. Shall we have limits on card-playing ability too? We could win money off this chap."

Tabitha said, "Now you are being ridiculous." She was about ready to stomp away. How would she endure an entire carriage ride of the same?

"But truly, sister." Edward gathered all the sticks and balls. "He is to join our family, be one of the brothers. We must make certain he will be a good fit."

"And respect you." Henry's eyes showed deep sympathy. "I too am roped into this. Not all gentlemen behave as a gentleman should. And we are here to make sure you don't have to converse with any of those other sorts."

"I do have a chaperone."

Oscar returned the balls to the table and smacked one into a pocket. "Who? Mrs. Hemming?" He laughed. "She'll be asleep against the wall."

Tabitha was secretly pleased that was the case. All this hovering was beginning to smother her. She moved to leave.

Tauney joined her in the doorway. "Why are you all just sitting around? Let's load the carriage and be off!"

"At last!" Edward put away Oscar's stick. "You are as ridiculous as Prinny with your fashion nonsense."

AFTER AN INTERMINABLE RIDE in the carriage—and one night in a respectable inn—they at last arrived in front of the Countess du Breven's home in a deluge of rain. The front approach itself took twenty minutes, wheels slogging through wet shale.

And now the great expanse of her lovely house stretched in front of them.

Tabitha lifted the covering over their window to see the approach to the estate. Beech trees lined their entry, limbs bent under the weight of the torrent, but the water brought out a lovely shade of pink in the shale rock of the drive. The whole scene felt other-worldly, and for the first time, a measure of hope rose within her when thinking of the party. "I do love Somerstone Manor." She longed to get lost on the grounds, walking among the flowers and hedges in the countess' expansive gardens.

Mrs. Hemming snored in the corner.

"As long as we can get out of this carriage, I don't care where we stay." Oscar sat stiffly, wedged and jostled against his brothers. Rain pounded the roof, their mounts followed behind. Four broad-shouldered, impatient, and damp men sat pinned together, forced to ride inside once the rain commenced.

They arrived in the hall, shaking water off their persons, the brothers forming a line to Tabitha's front, Henry at her side.

The Countess stepped forward. "We are so happy you have come, Lord Easton." She held out her hand, and Edward bowed over it. The others bowed with him, and Tabitha lowered in a deep curtsey.

Three gentlemen caught Tabitha's eye, coming down the stairs. Anthony Pemberton, one of the Pinkerton twins, and Reginald Beauchamp: three of the most sought after men in the *ton*, all in one place. "Oh. My. I wonder who else the countess has included in her invitations."

Edward followed her gaze and immediately bristled. "Brothers. As soon as we change, let us meet in my room to receive our assignments."

Tabitha sighed.

Henry placed his hand on hers. "Will you be all right? I believe I've been summoned elsewhere."

"Yes, quite." She indicated Mrs. Hemming, who was already bustling her away to get out of her wet things before she caught a chill.

Many eyes watched her move up the stairs. Accustomed to attention, she did not let it rattle her too much. But she would have much preferred a smaller gathering.

Reginald Beauchamp approached on the stairway, flipping his hair away to reveal a brilliant pair of green eyes. She held out her hand. "Hello, Mr. Beauchamp. Pleased to see you again." He was more handsome than any man deserved to be. A pity his attention never focused very long in one direction.

He bowed, and his kiss lingered on her gloved hand.

"Come child. We must get you warmed." Mrs. Hemming scowled at poor Mr. Beauchamp.

He raised his eyebrow in amusement then turned back to Tabitha. "Will I be seeing you at dinner?"

"Yes, she is going to eat, now if you'll excuse us."

"Mrs. Hemming, really." Deep embarrassment filled her. After the discomfort of travel and the slipping sense of control over her life, the emotion almost overwhelmed her. Grasping for something, any decision completely her own, in a moment of pure rebellion, she stepped closer to Mr. Beauchamp, quirked her lips in a half grin.

"Unless you want to meet sooner."

His eyes flew open in shock. Then he recovered, a teasing glint lighting his face.

"You surprise me."

To read the rest of Tabitha's Folly, Click HERE. OR go to Jen's Amazon page to order your copy.

ABOUT THE AUTHOR

An award winning author, including the GOLD in Foreword INDIES Book of the Year Awards, Jen Geigle Johnson discovered her passion for England while kayaking on the Thames near London as a young teenager.

She once greeted an ancient turtle under the water by grabbing her fin. She knows all about the sound a water-ski makes on glassy water and how to fall down steep moguls with grace. During a study break date in college, she sat on top of a jeep's roll bars up in the mountains and fell in love.

Now, she loves to share bits of history that might otherwise be forgotten. Whether in Regency England, the French Revolution, or Colonial America, her romance novels are much like life is supposed to be: full of adventure. She is a member of the RWA, the SCBWI, and LDStorymakers. She is also the chair of the Lonestar.Ink writing conference.

Follow her Newsletter HERE.

https://www.jengeiglejohnson.com

Twitter--@authorjen

Instagram--@authorlyjen

Made in the USA
Lexington, KY
13 July 2019